Breaking Up Is Hard to Do

Breaking Up Is Hard to Do

Ed Gorman

THORNDIKE
CHIVERS

This Large Print edition is published by Thorndike Press®,
Waterville, Maine USA and by BBC Audiobooks, Ltd,
Bath, England.

Published in 2004 in the U.S. by arrangement with
Carroll & Graf Publishers, a division of Avalon Publishing
Group, Inc.

Published in 2004 in the U.K. by arrangement with
Carroll & Graf Publishers.

U.S. Hardcover 0-7862-6498-5 (Mystery)
U.K. Hardcover 1-4056-3011-6 (Chivers Large Print)
U.K. Softcover 1-4056-3012-4 (Camden Large Print)

The text of this Large Print edition is unabridged.
Other aspects of the book may vary from the original edition.

Set in 16 pt. Plantin by Minnie B. Raven.

Printed in the United States on permanent paper.

British Library Cataloguing-in-Publication Data available

Library of Congress Cataloging-in-Publication Data

Gorman, Edward.
    Breaking up is hard to do / Ed Gorman.
    p. cm.
    ISBN 0-7862-6498-5 (lg. print : hc : alk. paper)
    1. McCain, Sam (Fictitious character) — Fiction.
  2. Private investigators — Iowa — Fiction.
  3. Mistresses — Crimes against — Fiction. 4. Cuban
Missile Crisis, 1962 — Fiction. 5. Nuclear bomb shelters
— Fiction. 6. Iowa — Fiction. 7. Large type books.
I. Title.
PS3557.O759B74 2004
813′.54—dc22   2004047921

JY   '04

TO THE JACKSON FAMILY

Steve, Phil, Ellen

And in memory of Peg and Jack

ACKNOWLEDGMENT

For the tenacious first editor who
Keeps me honest and keeps me
laughing —

Mindy Jarusek

"It's impossible to make people today understand what the Cuban Missile Crisis was like for the average American, Russian and Cuban. Nuclear holocaust was very much a real possibility. And it could have happened at any moment."

— Sloane Winthrop

October 24, 1962

ONE

He didn't call ahead for an appointment. He didn't knock. He just eased himself through my partially opened office door and said, "I've got a little business for you, Mr. McCain. I mean, if you're interested."

He scared me. When I describe him you'll wonder what I'm talking about. How somebody his size and his manner could scare me. I'm no tough guy but I was surely tougher than he was. And yet I got spooked because he was so odd, so wrong somehow.

There was something unclean about him, dusty, that pale complexion, those dead grey eyes, the heavy black topcoat that fit him hobo-like. And yet it wasn't frayed or dirty. And the voice that wasn't much more than a whisper. I'd heard that a lot after both wars. Men who'd had their throats and larynxes damaged. He was a black-and-white photo in an old, old book come mysteriously to life.

And in case you think this spectral appearance took place during a window-rattling midnight thunderstorm — it was eight-thirty a.m. on a sunny October day.

He held up a small package the size of a cigar box. It had been wrapped with manila paper and sealed with Scotch tape.

"It's an easy two hundred and fifty dollars, Mr. McCain. I just want you to deliver this to somebody."

"Gee, I'm really not a courier service."

"I know what you are, Mr. McCain. I checked you out."

"I'm not sure I like that."

"You check out people all the time."

"It's my job."

"Maybe it's my job, too."

I nodded to the package. "What's in the box?"

"That's irrelevant. It's nothing that can hurt anybody. Not physically, anyway."

"And why can't you deliver this package yourself?"

"I have my personal reasons." He hesitated. He was a hesitant man.

He pushed his rimless glasses up his small freckled nose and smiled. "It involves a woman. She —" He paused. He sat in front of the desk in my dusty little law office; maybe five foot five and 125 pounds and a sort of squint half the time. He

12

glanced at the framed degrees of law on the wall. "I don't think I've ever heard of a lawyer who was also a private investigator."

I'd gotten to the office early because I had to be at the courthouse at ten this morning and wanted to clear my desk of paperwork that was piling up. They warn you about a lot of things in law school but somehow they never get around to paperwork.

He sat. He squinted. He sniffled. He said, "Allergies."

"Ah."

He'd brought in a briefcase, which he now lifted and sat on his lap. He opened it, delved inside and pulled out what appeared to be an 8 x 11 black-and-white glossy photograph like those that celebrities hand out. Somewhere in a box I have several glossies like that of Gene Autry and Roy Rogers. They're autographed. I have a glossy of Lassie, too. She didn't autograph hers.

He handed me the photograph. I looked at it and said, "You ever see the movie *Laura*?"

"Many times. And I know just what you're going to say."

"You do?"

"Of course. You looked at her just now

13

for the first time and you're intrigued. Just the way Dana Andrews was intrigued."

I smiled. "A movie fan."

"Very much so."

"Who is she?"

"It doesn't matter."

"Then why show me the photo?"

"I wanted you to see who you'd be delivering the package to."

"I haven't agreed to deliver anything yet."

"What's in the package doesn't matter and she doesn't matter."

"I'd have to know more than that."

His eyes scanned my office again. "No offense, Mr. McCain, but you don't look awfully successful."

"I pay my bills every month."

"You can use the money. And for the money I'm offering, you'd be foolish to turn it down. And in checking you out, I didn't get the impression you're foolish."

I was thinking of what I could do with the money. It represented about a third of my monthly income. I didn't care for him or the reason he wanted to hire me but delivering a package probably couldn't get me in a whole lot of trouble.

"You couldn't deliver it yourself, huh?"

"It'd be more dramatic if somebody else delivered it."

"Western Union'd be a lot cheaper than two hundred and fifty dollars."

"Western Union — anybody can use Western Union. This has to be special, Mr. McCain. You're a movie fan. I don't have to tell you how a dramatic gesture can get to a woman."

"She break your heart, did she?"

He laughed. It was an unpleasant sound somehow. "Something like that." He tapped the box. "She goes out during the day but you can catch her at home tonight."

"She works?"

"Yes, but I'm not sure where. That's why night is safer."

I stood up. "What's your name?"

"Hastings."

"You have a first name?"

"You know you need the money, Mr. McCain."

I snapped my finger. "Peter Lorre."

"I used to consider that an insult. The older I get, I don't mind so much. Better I remind you of a movie star than just some nobody." Then: "I'm in a hurry, Mr. McCain." He stood up, closed his briefcase. Extracted from his overcoat a white number 10 envelope. No writing on the front. "Twelve twenties and two fives." He

15

shoved the envelope over to me.

I stared at it and then picked it up.

He said, "I need it delivered tonight, Mr. McCain." He pulled his briefcase from the desk. Walked to the door. "You've made me want to see *Laura* again. Too bad it's not showing somewhere around here."

Then he was gone. I picked up the envelope and counted the money, way too much money for so little work. Way too much.

TWO

"All we can do is plead guilty and hope for the best, Lumir."

"Tell 'er I was framed."

"That's crazy, Lumir," I said. "You were driving drunk. And you were alone. How could I say you were framed?"

"Maybe somebody slipped somethin' in my drink."

"C'mon, Lumir. We don't want to screw around. This is your second drunken driving charge."

"I seen this here show on the TV."

"Uh-huh."

"Where they claimed this guy went batshit for a while and couldn't be held responsible. What's that called?"

"I think you had it right, Lumir. I think that's the technical term for it. Going batshit."

Lumir of the sleeveless catsup-and-mustard-stained T-shirt said, "It is?"

" 'Temporary insanity' is what it's called,

Lumir. And we don't have a chance. Now shut up and let's go inside."

"You tell me t'shut up one more time, McCain, and I'm gonna throw you through a window."

"And here I was going to invite you to my birthday party, Lumir. My mom said I could invite all my extra-special friends." When you're the least successful lawyer in town, you usually get the dregs for clients. Lumir hadn't worked up to the dreg level yet. He still had miles to go before he slept.

I tried to walk off my time with Lumir. My little town has a good number of nooks and crannies dating back to the time when the Mesquakie Indians still roamed the prairies and when Thanksgiving was a communal feast in the Presbyterian church. There was, believe it or not, some peremptory coal mining, so a short-haul railroad was built, the roundhouse of which is now the town market; and there was a blacksmith's barn so big that they had square dances there twice a month. The barn had been refurbished a couple times since it had been built. We wanted to hang on to it.

Two blocks from my office I saw Abe

Leifer suddenly tap his chest and sit down quickly on the edge of a bus bench. Abe is the State Farm insurance agent. He's handled my family's insurance since the day my older brother — now alas long dead — was born.

"Abe? Abe? You all right?"

Abe was in his late fifties. You usually saw him in one of three brown sportcoats, each subtly different from the other, a white tab-collared shirt and brown slacks. He was a nice-looking man the local barbers always pointed to as an illustration of "a beautiful head of hair."

Right now, he was pale, sweaty and breathing hard.

"I got to lose some weight, Sam."

He had put on maybe thirty pounds in the last five years or so. Between his fingers, a Winston burned. Extra weight and cigarettes and middle age are not a good combination.

Just about everybody liked Abe. He'd been wounded twice in the war and as a result spent time occasionally in the Veterans hospital in Iowa City.

A few people stopped to see how he was doing.

"How's he doing?"

"You doing okay there, Abe?"

19

"Did you fall down or something, Abe?"

"Is he all right, Sam? What happened here?"

I became Abe's de facto press representative.

"He's fine."

"He just got a little winded is all."

"He works too hard. You know Abe."

Etc. and etc.

During the course of fifteen minutes, he got his wind and his color back. He started to look the way he should. But I still didn't want to leave him alone. Especially after I saw him try to stand up. His knees were wobbly.

"We're going for a little walk, Abe."

"Where?"

"The hospital. Two short blocks away."

"Sam, Sam, I'm fine. I just got winded is all. I don't need any hospital."

"You have a choice, Abe. You can walk beside me or I'll carry you and people'll think you're my bride."

"Sam, Sam —"

But he went.

I took him to the emergency room. While I waited for them to call his wife Helen and check him out, I wandered down the hall where I saw Peggy Leigh and Deirdre Murdoch standing outside an office marked Volunteers.

Peggy Leigh, who always tells you as part of her introduction that she's not the singer Peggy Lee, is well known in town for being able to get everybody of whatever status to give time or money to the hospital volunteer office. She's one of those short, square-yet-attractive women whose severe gazes can melt steel if need be. You never see her in anything but her uniform which is a blue blazer, white blouse, lighter blue skirt, hose, and flats.

She smiled and said, "Deirdre. Watch out for this guy. He has a way with women. Especially when he gets you in that car of his."

"I've got a neat new car myself," Deirdre said. "The only trouble is, I have to share it with my Mom. Dad won't let her have her own car." She smiled. "She does tend to get into accidents."

The phone rang inside the office. Deirdre excused herself and rushed into the office.

"She's getting off early today so she's working extra hard," Peggy said. "She works plenty hard as it is." Then: "Pretty, no?"

"Very."

"And Daddy rich."

"Very. The one and only Ross Murdoch."

"Our next governor."

"Maybe," I said.

"Oh, you Democrats. When will you admit that this is a Republican state?" She was also a tireless Republican volunteer.

"The state's changing, Peggy. Won't be Republican much longer."

Just then I saw Helen Leifer rush into the emergency room.

"Well, I need to go."

"Nice to see you, Sam."

Helen came over to me and took my hand. Her entire body was shaking. "Thanks for being such a good friend, Sam." She was a sweet-faced little woman bundled up inside a massive tan storm coat that she'd bought at Monkey Wards. I knew that because my mother had one just like it.

Then she was rushing away.

A few minutes after I got back from the hospital, the phone rang.

"Dawdling?" said Judge Esme Anne Whitney, the district magistrate for whom I investigate things.

"Doodling, actually." And I was. I'd returned a phone call and in the process begun penciling out a sketch of President Lincoln. For some reason, his is the only face I can draw that remotely resembles somebody human.

"Well, I hope you're better at dawdling than doodling."

"You're in an awfully chipper mood, this afternoon, Judge. Did something terrible happen to Chief Sykes?"

"Nothing terrible ever happens to Sykes. The terrible things are the things that Sykes does to our town."

The Judge is part of a large, rich Eastern family that came out here to Black River Falls, Iowa about a hundred years ago after a litigious argument with the Treasury Department over what it considered some rather — what is the word I want here? — illegal financial maneuverings. Disgraced, the family put some of its remaining millions into building our little town of 25,000 souls. Everything went fine with their Iowa empire here until WWII when the Sykes family, which had come to Black River Falls with the Southern migration of the late last century, got some federal contracts to start building roads and airstrips for the government. The Sykeses, through thrift and theft, made a few million dollars for themselves. And proceeded, before the

Whitneys quite understood what was going on, into bribing virtually every local official, bank and prominent merchant into supporting the Sykes slate of candidates.

While the Judge had her millions and her district court, she no longer had the sort of imperious power her family had become accustomed to.

Police Chief Clifford Sykes, Jr. is thus her enemy. It helps that he's none too bright, marginally crooked, and eager to wrap up major criminal cases before doing any serious investigating. I haven't kept track, not being a petty sort of person, but I believe that we've proven him wrong on the last eight murder cases that fell in his jurisdiction. He doesn't like us any better than we like him.

"I told a friend of mine you'd help him this afternoon."

"Is this one of your country club friends? Do I have to unload gold bullion again?"

"In fact, McCain, he *is* one of my country club friends. One of my nearest and dearest, in case you're interested. But I don't know what he wants. He just asked if I could get you out there as soon as possible."

"Who's this friend?"

"Ross Murdoch."

"The guy who's running for governor?"

"Yes."

"Why would somebody as rich and successful as he is want me in his mansion?"

"No offense, McCain, but that's the very question I asked him."

"Why would I take offense at that, Judge? Gosh, I know I'm a low-born swine."

"This is no time for being cute, McCain. He sounded sort of — strained. But then who wouldn't be with the election this close. Everybody's pulling for him but with all that left-wing money flooding the state, who knows what'll happen."

By "left-wing money," the Judge means money given by labor unions, teachers' unions, and any other groups that try to help the downtrodden and despised. You know, the scum of the earth.

"I can't get out there for a while."

"Well, I'm going to lean on you a little here and play boss. I want you to get out there as soon as you can. I don't like to hear my good friends agitated this way." She lighted a cigarette, something she does to the tune of two packs a day. "He was so excited about his fancy new bomb shelter the last few weeks. He seems to have forgotten all about it now. Get out there as quickly as you can, McCain."

All this is taking place during what the press had come to call the Cuban Missile Crisis. For the past four days a confrontation had been building.

And now it was a crisis. Jack Kennedy had proof that Khrushchev was on the cusp of installing Russian missiles on Cuban soil. Missiles that could easily reach America. So Kennedy had now set up a naval blockade and essentially dared Khrushchev to try and run it. The world didn't want to think about what Khrushchev would do. The prospect of nuclear war had frozen everybody in place. You went to work, you played with your kids, you made whoopee with your wife, you paid your bills, you raked beautiful Indian-summer leaves. But no matter where you went or what you did, the subject of the missile crisis was there. If you didn't bring it up, a friend did. In television interviews teachers explained how difficult it was to make children understand what was going on without giving them nightmares.

I'd grown up with air raid drills, with duck-and-cover, with movie and TV melo-dramas inspired by good old Uncle Joe McCarthy. According to him, there were more commies in the US of A than there were Americans. I'd had plenty of night-mares myself. But all that had been nothing more than practice. This could well be the nuclear war, the nuclear holo-caust, the nuclear winter we had been dreading ever since 1945.

During the past four or five years, bomb shelters had become popular. Most people couldn't afford anything fancy. They'd find a spot in their basement that could be walled off with brick or concrete block or some other fortification and then just kind of hope for the best. Most of these home-made shelters were worthless. When the nukes hit, you needed to be in some place deep and well protected.

People like Ross Murdoch, who had the wherewithal to have their shelters profes-sionally built, just might survive for a time in their shelters. They'd been designed by architects who followed government guide-lines, and they'd been built by construction men and carpenters who knew what they were doing.

The day was warm, bright, smoky with autumn haze in the piney hills. Hard to be-lieve that all the houses, stores, schools, roads and so on could be turned into ash and rubble in an hour or two. The older you get, I'm told, the more the idea of your own extinction becomes easier to grasp, if not make your peace with. But the extinction of virtually everybody and everything you've grown up with? Now that was a tough one. A damned tough one. I found myself saying little fragments of prayers, something I hadn't done in a while.

Ross Murdoch lived in a brick house that was half-hidden behind huge fir trees. I parked my red '51 Ford ragtop in front of the front steps, got out and walked up the steps to the door.

I looked out over the land surrounding the house. Pine trees and carefully landscaped grass. A high meadow with horses, the color of chestnuts; a green John Deere in a distant field that was hauling a wagon full of new trees to be planted; and a leg of river that looked silver-blue in the sunlight. The aromas of autumn were every bit as alluring as the colors of autumn. It was one of those sweet soft days when you wished you were a bird. Or at least somebody who didn't have to work.

I heard a voice say "Hello? May I help you?" and when I turned around I saw a young woman in a white blouse and black slacks leaning against the doorframe. She was watching me with obvious amusement.

Then, "Oh. Hi. We almost met at the hospital." Then, "You're easily distracted, I take it?"

"Distracted?" She was the young woman who'd been talking to volunteer Peggy Leigh. She certainly got your attention.

"You knock on the door and then turn around and get so caught up in the sights that you forget all about the knock."

"Guilty as charged."

A gamin grin. She put forth a slender but strong hand. "I'm Deirdre Murdoch."

"Sam McCain."

"C'mon in, Sam. Dad's in the den." Then: "Oh, how do you like my car?"

I'd noticed the sleek new yellow foreign machine as I'd wheeled into the driveway. "Italian?"

"British."

"I'm not up on my foreign cars but it's a beaut, that's for sure."

The interior of the house had the feel of a museum about it. Everything fought for your attention and approval. The number of rooms seemed countless. Each room I glimpsed on the way down the parqueted main corridor looked like a furniture display in an expensive Chicago store.

"I'm not sure why he wants you here. He's just very —" She looked troubled herself. "Did you ever see *Invasion of The Body Snatchers?*"

"One of my three all-time favorite movies."

"Really?"

"Absolutely."

"Well, Dad's been like one of the pod people lately. And today — I'd swear he wasn't my father at all."

She was a beauty, I suppose, but there was a freckled, young-girl vividness about that sweet little face and that great gleaming gash of a smile that overwhelmed you when she glanced over at you.

"Mom's very upset, too. Whatever's bothering him, he's keeping it to himself. At first I thought it might be the bomb shelter. You know how it is when you get things built. It's never very smooth. And a lot of things went wrong with the shelter. It wasn't anybody's fault, really. It's just that Dad's a perfectionist. He wanted to make the shelter into a place he could go to be absolutely alone. Drink a beer or two and watch some TV. Or play some of his old Louie Armstrong records. He loves Dixieland jazz. It just got finished a couple of days ago. Mom and I were hoping that that would make him happy. But it didn't. He's just kept on — brooding. That's the only word I can think of."

"The campaign's got to be taking its toll on him by now."

"I know. But — but this is like a personality change. Like a pod person." We walked up to the door of the den. She knocked once and then opened the door.

The den was a sanctuary of wall-to-wall books, several Vermeer lithographs, genuine Persian rugs, a desk a fighter jet could land on, and so much leather furniture the cattle population must have been seriously depleted when the manufacturer was putting it together. The sunlight angling through the window gave the wide, deep room a serenity that belied all those dead animal eyes staring at me.

Ross Murdoch was a slender six-footer in a white shirt, blue slacks and cinnamon-colored cowboy boots. He was handsome in a conventional middle-aged way. He didn't try to prove his masculinity with his handshake, which I appreciated, and he spoke quietly when he offered me a chair. "Care for a drink?"

"No thanks, Mr. Murdoch."

" 'Ross.' "

"No thanks, Ross."

"And 'Sam's' okay?"

"Sam's fine."

"I'll be down at the stables, Dad."

"Thanks, honey."

"Nice to meet you, Sam," she said and sounded as if she really meant it. Then she was gone.

I sat in one of the deep leather chairs. He sat, somewhat anxiously, on the edge of his enormous desk. He raised himself up on one side and dug something out of his front pocket. He flipped it in the air toward me. I caught it. A silver dollar.

"That's when money was money," he said.

"My early birthday present?"

"The Judge told me you were a smart-ass. Usually, I don't mind smart-asses but unfortunately now's not the time. As you'll see." He took a very deep breath and then a very deep drink from the bourbon-filled glass he had on his desk. "The silver dollar's to hire you. Lawyer-client. I've got a check for a thousand dollars for you in my desk with your name on it. I want you to look at something for me."

First I get two hundred and fifty dollars for delivering a letter and now I was being offered $1000 to look at something. I was going to be small-town rich. Or at least small-town comfortable. I started mentally listing all the bills I could pay off.

"That's a lot of money."

"You're going to earn it."

"Doing what exactly?"

He got up and started walking around, sometimes facing me, sometimes not. Sometimes he seemed to be talking to me, at others he seemed to be talking to himself.

"Sam, I'm going to withdraw from the governor's race."

"Are you serious?"

"Afraid I am." He pressed slender fingers to his forehead as if he had a headache. "I've made my peace with it. I don't like it but I don't have any choice."

"Have you talked it over with anybody yet?"

"Not yet. The Judge puts a lot of faith in your skill and integrity."

News to me, I thought.

"What I need now is legal advice."

"I don't mean to be immodest but there are sure more experienced lawyers than me around."

"Yes. But I don't trust them. I need somebody I can have absolute trust in. Maybe later on I'll hire some additional lawyers. But for right now I want a sensible, homegrown young man with the kind of credentials Esme says you have."

"Well, I'm flattered. But —"

He held his hand up to stop me from speaking. "We have something in common. Cliffie Sykes. He hates me because Judge Whitney is one of my best friends. He's tried to arrest me on four different occasions for minor infractions of the law — and I've beaten him very publicly at his own game. He always said he'd get even and now — well, now he may have a chance." Then: "Sure you wouldn't want a drink?"

"I'm fine."

He walked over to a dry bar and took care of his glass again. He added a spritz of water. He turned back to me and said, "This time I may have handed myself over to him."

"You've lost me."

He started pacing again. "Have you heard about my bomb shelter?"

"I think everybody in town has."

"Well, it's all true. A big room that's half living room with the other half being bunk beds enough for twelve. Comfortable beds."

"I'd like to see it."

"You will. In just a few minutes. But right now I need your word that everything I say is between us."

"Lawyer-client privilege."

"Sam, I'm not going to elaborate on what I want you to do for me. I need you to check things out for yourself. I need you to go down to the bomb shelter and look it over and then come back upstairs. Then we'll talk and I'll tell you what I know."

The right side of his mouth had developed a tiny tic. His long slender left hand twitched twice.

"You like things mysterious, Ross."

"I'll explain everything — afterward."

"That's what you hired me for? To look in your bomb shelter?"

"That's one of the reasons, Sam. The other reason — well, you'll find out for yourself."

"I can't ask any questions?"

"Not right now. Just please do what I ask, Sam. Please."

I wondered if Deirdre was at the door. Listening. Probably. I would be, if he was my father. I didn't yet know what was wrong but I could sense that despite his apparent self-control, he was coming apart in little ways. Little ways that would lead to a complete loss of self-control very soon now.

Deirdre, as I'd suspected, was walking away very quickly — too quickly — when I opened the door. She disappeared into shadows near the front door.

At this point, he was sighing every thirty seconds or so. Quick, ragged sighs that just might portend a heart-attack. Maybe his body would turn on itself and kill him.

He walked to a door, opened it. "Down the stairs. The various rooms are marked. You won't have any trouble finding it."

"You're not going down there with me?"

Another sigh. "I'd prefer not to." Even his hand was glazed with sweat now. It shone like the brass doorknob it held.

Deirdre came up. "Want me to go with him, Dad?"

"No!" He said it with such anger that he sounded like a different person entirely. "I need you to stay out of this, Deirdre. I've told you that already."

"Want me to go to my room and play with dolls or something, Dad?" She was now as angry as he'd been. She obviously didn't like being treated so coldly, especially in front of a guest. But she was quick to relent. "I was just trying to help, Dad."

Now it was his turn to sound apologetic. "I'm sorry, honey. It's just — things." He couldn't even finish the sentence. "All this'll be over soon. I'm sure Sam here can help me."

Deirdre and I looked at each other. Her expression was much like mine. I wasn't quite sure what would "all be over soon." The answer was apparently in the bomb shelter. As to what I'd be "helping" him with, I had no idea.

"I guess I will go upstairs, actually," Deirdre said, the brown eyes melancholy. Easy to picture her as a little girl confused and disappointed by the secret world of adults. "Well, good luck, Sam."

"Thanks."

"Hope I see you again, Sam."

"I'll make a point of it."

When she'd gone, he said, "You made a friend. Her fiancé broke off their engagement a little over a year ago. This is the first time I've seen her show any interest in a male since then."

"Well, I know one other male she sure seems to care about."

"Oh?"

"You. That's pretty easy to see."

"Yes," he said, being mysterious again. "And that sure doesn't make any of this any easier, either." Then: "Here, Sam. Down these stairs and to the right you'll find the bomb shelter."

THREE

The basement steps were spiral-style. And steep. I was about halfway down them, when the whole thing started to feel unreal. He was scared to the point of dysfunction. He wanted to pay me a thousand dollars but wouldn't say why. And now he wanted me to check out his bomb shelter.

The basement was divided into rooms with doors. I was in a basement unlike any I'd ever seen before. Usually there's a sink and washer where Mom does the laundry. And a coal bin left over from Grandpa's day. And a furnace that sounds like a bomb blast every time it comes on. And in the various corners are stacks of magazines running from *Colliers* to *The Saturday Evening Post* and wooden cases of empty Pepsi bottles. And then you've got your galvanized buckets and your mops that look like gray seaweed and your collection of ancient dusty cleaning fluids. And all sorts of other stuff that should've been thrown out long ago but somehow never was. The smells would be laundry soap, dust, dampness, and mildew from the stacks of newspapers. You would see an occasional bug, an occasional crack in the floor, an occasional cobweb on the unfinished ceiling.

Not so in Ross Murdoch's basement.

The basement was laid out in a maze of narrow hallway, walls and doors. It smelled of the fresh lime green paint on the walls and of the air conditioning that really wasn't necessary on an Indian summer day like this one. There were no bugs, no cracks in the floor and, God forbid, no cobwebs. Each door was marked with a neatly painted sign. FURNACE ROOM, LAUNDRY ROOM, and two others. BOMB SHELTER was what I was looking for and BOMB SHELTER was what I found.

The shelter was pretty much as it had been described. Very good living room and kitchen furnishings took up half of it; the other half offering six sets of bunk beds and a couple huge armoires. In the kitchen area there were enough boxes and crates of canned foodstuffs to keep a small army going for a year or so. Same with cigarettes, cigars, soda pop and alcoholic refreshments. There was a large carpet that looked to be the indoor-outdoor stuff that would hold up for a while. And the electrical generator in the east corner was imposing both for its size and its fire-engine red color. There were plenty of lamps, a portable 17-inch TV and a large Zenith radio that had so many buttons it could probably tune in Mars if you wanted it to. Home sweet home.

The dead woman spoiled everything.

She was sprawled on the brown corduroy-covered couch. Arms flung wide, silver silk blouse torn to reveal small breasts contained in a white bra, blue skirt pushed up to mid-thigh. She wore blue hose and silver flats. She had wonderful flawless legs. The purple bruising on her neck likely showed the means of her death. Some murder victims look horrible, their expressions reflecting clearly the terrors and suffering they went through. Other corpses appear almost peaceful. As if their passing had not been all that bad; or as if their passing had been something that they might have secretly wished for.

If the young woman's skin hadn't just now given a trace of the blue tint that would soon invade it, you'd have thought she was just resting, waiting to be called to dinner.

Her face was the most interesting part of

the picture, not because it was so beautiful, which it was, but because it belonged to the young woman whose black-and-white glossy Hastings had shown me earlier this morning.

I walked the length of the room. Cliffie wouldn't search it properly so I assumed it would fall to me. I spent twenty minutes down there. I imagined Ross Murdoch was wondering what I was doing. But he was scrupulous about staying out of my way. He'd looked scared enough to put me in charge, something he probably wasn't used to. Everything about him spoke to being the king of the walk.

I didn't find anything remarkable. I'd been hoping for something obvious. A button. A footprint. A note saying: "Yes, I killed her. Here's my home phone number. I'll be waiting for your call."

But no such luck. Police science would have to take over from here. Cliffie had a recent graduate of the Police Academy as his number two now. He wasn't a genius but he was competent and if Cliffie let him do his job — "Who cares about all this mumbo-jumbo!" I'd heard Cliffie snap at the guy one night — he might actually come up with some interesting ideas.

Now it was time to go back upstairs.

★ ★ ★

"You'll have to tell me everything, Ross. Everything. That's the only way I can help you."

He didn't say anything. He just sat slumped behind his desk. He just looked sad, scared. I wondered if he was in shock.

I leaned forward, put my elbows on the front of the desk and looked right at him. "Who was she, Ross? I already know who she is. But I want to hear you say it. And then I want to hear you say that she was your girlfriend."

"Her name is Karen Hastings. She wasn't *my* girlfriend. She was *our* girl-friend."

"What?"

"Three of my best friends from here — we went to a business convention in Chicago. She was a hostess in a booth. We all got drunk together — and more than once — over the four days we were there." The men in his group were, like many men their age who'd taken Jack Kennedy as an icon, into sailing, hot air ballooning and, inevitably, a mean game of touch football.

"Meaning you four and the woman?"

"Yes. And then we decided — you know how things can sound perfectly sensible when you're drunk — that we all needed some excitement in our lives but that running around on the side was too risky. But what if we all chipped in and set up a mistress in a nice apartment not far from where we lived? Shared the expenses and shared the woman. This was two years ago. Before I'd decided to run for governor."

"I think the word you want here is *prostitute*."

"Yes. But of a very special kind. So anyway, we all pitched in and arranged for a very nice apartment and for a monthly allowance and for a clothing allowance. We even paid for her life insurance. And to have her visit a doctor every two months."

"She liked the idea?"

He laughed but without pleasure. "She loved it. We didn't find out why till later. She was wanted by the Chicago police for extortion."

I sat back in my chair. "This is about the dumbest idea I've ever heard of."

"There were a couple stories just like it back east. That's where we got the idea. We just assumed we'd be better at it."

"And you didn't see any of the pitfalls?"

He shook his head. "You don't need to remind me, Sam. Right away there was jealousy among the men. Two of them developed crushes on her. One of them I think fell in love with her. And then there was the fact that she started seeing other men on the side. I didn't get jealous of that — the more I got to know her, the less I wanted to do with her — but I couldn't figure out what we were paying for. She was ours. We were paying her way."

"And then she started shaking you down."

He looked surprised. "God, she wanted more and more money all the time."

"That kind of arrangement, Ross. They always come back for more."

"She didn't wait for that. She said she'd contact my political enemies. Sell them the story. She changed. In Chicago she seemed so — sweet."

"She was planning this all along. The first time she probably didn't know how wealthy you were. Then she found out you were running for governor. You were going to be a very big payday for her."

"I knew that, of course. All I could think of was getting through the election."

"There's also a good chance that she would also have sold her story to your so-called enemies, anyway."

"Oh, God, you know I hadn't thought of that. You really think she would've done it?"

"I can't say for sure. But probably. How about the others? How much did she get from them?"

"The same for all of us. We divided all the payments by four." He tried a clumsy joke. "I wonder if you can divide a murder four ways."

"It'll be tough. You've got her body in the basement."

"I didn't put it there. I really didn't. And I certainly don't know who killed her."

Now it was my turn to get up and pace. I suppose that's sort of impolite, in somebody else's office and all, but I needed some kind of exercise suddenly. Sitting in the chair just made me realize how hopeless his situation was. For one thing, he might very well have killed her himself, put the body in the bomb shelter, and then concocted this fancy tale of "discovering" her down there. Surprise, surprise.

I went over to the window and looked out on the day. "I'm going to assume for the minute that you didn't kill her."

"Gee, thanks, Sam. I already said I didn't."

"As I said, I'm assuming that. But I'm not ruling it out."

"I didn't kill her, all right? I didn't kill her."

"Then that leaves two likely possibilities." I turned back to him. "One of your three friends killed her. Or somebody we don't know about. Yet."

"I'm going to let you call this one, Sam. That's why I got you out here."

I checked my watch. "Here's what you're going to do. You're going to call Cliffie and get him out here. Tell him you just discovered the body."

"But won't the coroner set the time of death?"

"Maybe. But even if he sets it five hours before you call Cliffie, all you have to say is that you didn't go down into the basement until right before you called."

He gazed up at me with glassy, dazed eyes. "It's funny. Being governor meant so much to me and now —"

I walked back toward his desk. "Right now your biggest concern has to be staying out of prison." I headed for the door. "You don't want Cliffie to think that you called me before you called him."

He just sat where he was, still slumped. "Call him, Ross," I said, "call him right now." I sounded as I were speaking to a naughty child.

FOUR

"I get down on my hands and knees every night and thank Khrushchev for being such a rotten, treacherous old bastard. Thanks to him this is the golden era of my sex life."

You've heard of Ernest Hemingway, F. Scott Fitzgerald, John Steinbeck. Everybody has.

But how about Brad Brand? Rod Randall? Ty Tolan? They're all writers, too. In fact, they're all the same guy, our little burg's only living professional dirty book writer, Kenny Thibodeau. Since Bible-thumping district attorneys across the land are trying to make political names for themselves sending "smut peddlers" to prison, everybody in the dirty book industry uses phony names these days.

There's no explicit sex in these books and good sturdy bourgeoisie morality always wins out in the end. The covers suggest otherwise, of course, and it is often the covers, some of which are excellent examples of commercial art, that these politically ambitious district attorneys rave on about. If you can churn them out quickly enough, and Kenny can, you can make a sort of living at writing them.

According to Kenny, it isn't easy to come up with *Hot Rod Harlots*, *Motel Minx* and *Surfin' Sinners* all in the same month without having your brain collapse.

"In the last eight days, I've slept with four girls who usually wouldn't piss on me if I was on fire," Kenny continued. "And it's all because they think we're going to get nuked by the commies."

Kenny himself has been mistaken for a commie by local members of such organizations as the American Legion, the Veterans of Foreign Wars, the Catholic Church, the Presbyterian Church and the Amish. You can also throw in several biker gangs, my parents, his parents and the parents of any girl he's ever dated. It's not the fact that he writes dirty books — that just makes him a deviate — it's the fact that he has a little black tuft of beard, a black beret, a black turtleneck sweater, black jeans, tan desert boots and a pair of thick-lensed black-rimmed glasses. He is, in other words, a stereotypical beatnik, our resident beatnik in fact. And as everybody knows, beatniks are — in addition to being smelly, profane, lazy and pretentious — commies.

We were in my office. I was looking over my phone notes that Jamie Newton had left behind during her two hour shift. Jamie's still in high school. I represented her father in a property dispute. He told me afterward that he couldn't afford to pay me so he'd give me his daughter for two hours a day as my secretary. In theory that sounded all right. But after seeing the first letter she ever typed for me — and after trying to decipher a couple of phone messages — I decided that she was his secret revenge. We'd lost the case. Jamie was my punishment and no matter how hard I begged, he wasn't going to break our deal. "Fair's fair," he always said. He wasn't taking her back.

Jamie returned from the john saying, "Turk didn't call, did he, Mr. C?"

On the Perry Como TV show, his regulars always refer to him as Mr. C. Thus Jamie refers to me as Mr. C. That my last name begins with M bothers her not at all. Turk is her boyfriend, who is a kind of parody juvenile delinquent, the kind you see in Hollywood movies. You know, the fierce bad boys in *West Side Story*.

Kenny ogled Jamie all the way to her typewriter. He took special note of how she seated herself. Jamie is the girl paperback cover artists have in mind whenever they're illustrating a "jail bait" novel. Though she dresses well thanks to earning free clothes as a department store model, she has a body that not even the primmest of dresses could disguise. Plus she's got a sweet sensual face that belies her body. She's actually innocent and decent and that's what you see in her blue blue eyes and her little-kid smile.

"No, he didn't call, I'm afraid."

"He had to go to traffic court this morning."

"Wasn't he just in traffic court a couple weeks ago?"

"Chief Sykes really has it in for him. He won't cut Turk any slack at all. Turk was just going thirty miles over the speed limit last night and Chief Sykes arrested him. He's got that big yellow Indian, you know. Turk says cops shouldn't be allowed to ride motorcycles because it puts drivers at a disadvantage. You know, when you're trying to outrun them."

"Nobody ever puts anything over on Turk," I said. "He's thinking all the time."

"He said he's going to say that in court

this morning, Mr. C. About the cops having the advantage with their motorcycles."

"That should get him ten to twenty on a chain gang," Kenny laughed. If Jamie understood what he meant, she didn't let on. She set to typing. That is, after she was done with her ritual. I figured at her fastest Jamie could type thirty words a minute, at least twenty of which were misspelled. In order to accomplish this amazing feat, certain things had to be in place. A fresh bottle of Pepsi with a long straw bobbing up inside the neck. A Winston cigarette burning uselessly in her pink plastic ashtray. And the latest issue of one of her teen magazines angled across the corner of her metal typing desk. The magazine was there, waiting and ready, for when she took one of her breaks.

I jerked my head at Kenny, indicating that we should go outside. My crowded, dusty little one-room office wasn't a place for exchanging confidential information.

"We're going down to the drug store for a Coke," I said to Jamie.

"Sure thing, Mr. C," she said, leaning over the typewriter and jamming down hard on a particular key.

"We'll be back in twenty minutes or so," I said.

"This darn thing. Is there a k in concern? I'm pretty sure it's c, isn't it?"

"You could always look at the one thousand spelling words book I got you. I'm sure you'll find 'concern' in there."

"Oh, yeah, right. That spelling book. I always forget about it. In fact —" And she began gaping around for it as if it might be playing hide-and-seek, "I haven't been able to find it lately. You think you could get me another one?"

Oh, yeah; her father was one sly guy. I lose his case and he gives me Jamie.

The only thing that had stayed the same at the Rexall drugstore was Mary Travers, whose name was now Mary Lindstrom. She was still possessed of the pale skin and dark hair and naturally pink mouth and soft blue gaze that I'd almost fallen in love with. She was the girl everybody said I should marry. Which I probably would've done if it hadn't been for my obsession with the beautiful Pamela Forrest. Mary had had the same kind of obsession with me. And for about the same length of time, starting in second grade.

She'd had two children rather quickly but still looked young and vital. Since her husband Wes owned the Rexall — he was a pharmacist who'd inherited the place from his father — she worked the counter sometimes. She was shy as ever. There had always been a sad erotic quality to her shyness and sometimes now when I saw her on the street I felt not only lust but loss. I'd probably made a bad choice in passing her by.

She served us our coffees quickly, too busy to say much. The place was crowded. I glanced around. They'd redecorated a year ago. Everything was new and bright and plastic. I missed the old ice cream chairs and the crooked paperback rack that squeaked when you turned it around and the booths where you could sit on Saturdays and watch all the girls come and go. The sandwich counter was the last vestige of the old place. The booths were gone, replaced by glass counters filled with everything from watches to perfumes. It's funny, isn't it, how we can get as sentimental about places as we do people? Sometimes I walk around this old town of ours and I'll see a hitching post where horses used to be tied, which I can still sort of remember. They kept them right up till the time of Korea. Or the grade school where I spent three years before they retired it in favor of a new red brick building. Or the ancient

Rialto theater where your parents never wanted you to go because there were supposedly rats lurking in every dark corner — but it only cost eight cents and the holy trinity could be seen there regularly, Gene and Roy and Hoppy. We call them inanimate, all these places of our youth, but they aren't really, not after we've invested them with memories and melancholy.

I said, "You want to make twenty bucks?"

"I get to play Shell Scott?"

"I thought you liked to play Mike Hammer."

"I've been reading a lot of Zen stuff, man. Mike Hammer is too violent."

"Maybe you should be Miss Marple."

"Very funny." He sipped his coffee. "Actually, I'd rather be Miss Marple than Hercule Poirot. He's such a little twit."

"Yeah; I like Miss Marple better, too."

"Maybe I'll be Philip Marlowe. I'm in a kind of Philip Marlowe mood lately."

"Whatever that means. Can we get back to the subject?"

"You want me to dig up dirt on — whom?"

Kenny Thibodeau could make a lot more money as an investigator than he does as a dirty book writer. But I suppose

it's a matter of prestige. Just about anybody can be a gumshoe but very few
among us could write *Nympho Nurses*.
Kenny knows, or knows how to get, information on virtually everybody in town. I
use him a lot. He really does like to play
private eye.

"Start with Ross Murdoch."

"You're kidding. He's going to be governor."

I didn't want to elaborate on that. "I'll
have some other names for you later. You'll
be busy for a while."

"Maybe get some material for a book.
I'm hoping one of these cases for you turns
up some really raunchy stuff one of these
days."

He slid off the stool. "I still miss that paperback rack. The old metal one."

"Yeah, so do I."

"That new layout they've got over
there — all those shelves and everything —
it's too respectable for people like us,
McCain."

"I agree."

"God, we're getting old, McCain."

"Yeah, our mid-twenties. We'll have
chrome walkers before you know it."

The way Mary kept glancing at me, I
knew she wanted to talk. I was happy to

wait around. In addition to somebody I daydreamed of sleeping with from time to time, she was pure, nice woman. She had to give up college when her dad got throat cancer. I never once heard her complain or feel sorry for herself.

"How've you been?" she said when the rush was over.

"About the same as the last time we talked. That was about fifteen years ago, right?"

She smiled. "Seems more like thirty. It's just going so fast. We'll actually be thirty one of these days. Do you ever think about it?"

"I'm too boyish to think about stuff like that." Then: "I think about it all the time."

She leaned forward and said, "Wes asked me for a divorce last week and I said yes. He met a lady pharmacist at a convention. He's been driving to Des Moines to see her." Her tone was flat. If she was sad about it, she hid it well.

"I'm sorry."

"I'm not sure I am, Sam. To be honest, I mean."

"You have any suspicions beforehand?"

"Yes. I mean, by the end it got to be obvious. It's funny — Pamela Forrest finally got her dream: you know, finally getting

Stu Grant to marry her and now I hear she's miserable. And Wes finally got his, getting to marry me, and now he's found someone else."

"So how do you feel about all this?"

She shrugged her slender shoulders. "Oh, you know, mixed feelings. It wasn't ever much of a marriage. You know how jealous he is about everybody. If I wasn't home doing housework or behind the counter here at the store, he was worried I was cheating on him. He accused me of it so much I almost called you a couple of times to make it true."

"I'm glad you didn't."

"So am I. I'm not the cheating type. He would've dragged me down with him."

"So now what?"

"Well, his father's really angry. His mother never liked me. Coming from the Hills the way I did . . . well, you know. She pretty much thought I was trash and that her precious Wes was marrying below his station. But his father and I always got along. He's kind of cranky at the store here but you should see him when he's with his two grandkids. One day he was so happy to be picking up Ellie, he just burst into tears."

"Man, that goes into 'Believe It Or Not.' "

57

"Right now, of course, they're pretty mad at Wes, too. He's pretty much taken over the pharmacy here. And they're embarrassed by what he's done. So they're making sure he gives me the house and the second car and a decent amount of child support. I'll keep working here with longer hours and they'll pay for all my insurance. Knowing Granddad, he'll also be buying clothes for the kids. He's always shopping for them."

A customer. Coffee and a Danish that was probably starting to dry out from the morning. But they're good that way. Just a tad bit old. I got one for myself. She spent ten minutes subduing the new crowd. Then came back to me.

She asked me how the woman I'd most recently dated was doing. "I heard she moved to Rochester."

"Well, I kind of thought that might turn into something. But she went up there so many times that she fell in love with her oncologist. They're getting married in six months." She'd been another girl I'd grown up with in the Hills, same as Mary and Pamela. She moved to Iowa City, worked her way through nursing school, and married a guy from Rock Island. Everything went reasonably well until she found out she had breast cancer. He couldn't handle it. He finally just ran away. We dated for a couple of months and it was fun. She is a very good woman. The sex was wonderful. But then she started talking about this oncologist in terms that weren't doctorly. How he reminded her a little of Tony Curtis. How he'd played quarterback at the U of Minnesota. How he had this really nifty frontier-style cabin on a lake up near the Canadian border. Wasn't too hard to figure out what was going on. We hadn't been in love. We'd been lonely and wanted to *think* we were in love but when she told me she'd decided to move up there, I think we were both relieved that our little charade was over.

"It's kind of funny, Sam."

"What is?"

"It's like we're starting all over again. Pamela's probably getting a divorce. I'm getting a divorce. And you're still just sort of wandering around."

"Starting all over," I said, thinking about it. In a way she was right; she was more right than wrong, anyway. And I wasn't sure that was good news. I was finally starting to grow up a little. I was even thinking of selling my rag-top. Showing up for court dates in a red hot rod had started to pall. Maybe a turd brown four-door Dodge sedan with a *Nixon in '64* bumper sticker would be more like it. And I could start wearing bow ties and boxer shorts and sock garters and . . . I hoped I never got that far gone. I always wanted to hear Buddy Holly singing in the back of my head. But I was getting older, no doubt about it. And the idea of a wife and kids didn't sound as alien as it once had.

"Well," I said, sliding off the stool. "Time to get back to the office."

She said, in her quiet way, "I'm glad we saw each other, Sam."

"Me, too."

Then somebody asked for a "refill on the java." Suddenly we were in a 1946 Monogram gangster movie. Java my ass.

On the walk back to my office, I heard somebody call my name. Turned out to be Jamie. "Had to get some girl stuff." She looked uncomfortable saying it. "I only took a couple of minutes off."

The shape of the small brown sack she carried, I figured it was Tampax.

"No problem, Jamie. Any calls?"

"Somebody named Hastings. He said it was important and he'd try you back."

I wondered if he knew about Karen yet. I doubted there had been time for the word to spread. Cliffie was probably still out at the Murdoch place. But it wouldn't be long now before the press was there and the story would make its way to the public.

"Turk had to leave," she said, as if this would come as bad news to me. "He's just such a gentleman. Have you ever noticed that?"

"Oh, yes," I said. "All the time."

"Like when I had to carry in all those heavy office supplies this morning."

"He helped you, huh?"

"No. He couldn't help me. On account of his bad back."

"Oh, I didn't know he *had* a bad back."

"Well, I actually didn't, either. He said he hurt it playing poker."

"You can hurt your back playing poker?"

"Turk says you can. From sitting so long."

"The poor dear," I said, even though sarcasm rarely registers with Jamie.

"But he was a gentleman about it, Mr. C. All the time I was carrying those boxes in, he sat in the front seat listening to the radio. And every time I kind of staggered past with a heavy load, you know what he did?"

"I'm afraid to hear."

"He apologized, Mr. C. Every single

61

time. He said, 'I'm sorry, babe. If I hadn't hurt my back playing poker, I'd be helping you right now with those boxes.' Now that's a real gentleman."

What do you say? I'm sure Mrs. Goebbels thought her son was a gentleman, too.

Jamie left soon after coming back from the bathroom. We said good night. I checked the phone answering service. No calls. Then I switched on the radio for the local news. Out here that means farm news, too, which isn't so bad. I know just enough about farming to understand how the markets are performing in Chicago on cattle, hogs, corn futures and so on. It's the farming commercials that get me. Most of them are too slick, farmers played by professional actors from back east. They all sound like they taught Latin at Rutgers and moonlighted playing farmers.

There was no news about Ross Murdoch finding a body in his bomb shelter. There was plenty of news about the naval blockade around Cuba. No Russian ships had been sighted yet. Not nearby, anyway. But many many nautical miles away three Russian ships could be seen. If they stayed their course, they would end up right in the center of the blockade. The White House, it was said, had no comment on these ships.

Because there wasn't anything I could do about Khrushchev and his dangerous and stupid ideas, I concentrated on Ross Murdoch. Why wasn't the news reporting on the body in his bomb shelter? The story should be all over everywhere. I spent ten minutes dialing around station to station. Nothing. Both the Cedar Rapids and Iowa City stations carried national and international news at this time. Eventually, this story would be carried on the national news segments.

I looked up Ross Murdoch's home phone number and called him.

A male voice said, "The Murdoch residence."

"This is Sam McCain. I was out there earlier today. I'd like to speak to Ross if I could."

"I'm sorry, Mr. McCain, he's in a meeting right now."

"Who's this, please?"

"This is Jim Gilliam. I'm handling Mr. Murdoch's press relations."

"I see. Exactly how long do you think it'll be before he gets out of that meeting?"

"I'm afraid I don't know. It's a very important meeting."

"I'll bet it is."

"I'll be happy to take your number if you'd like."

"No, thanks. I'll just try later."

"Well, thanks for calling, Mr. McCain." And hung up.

Political candidates had a lot of meetings. Ross Murdoch wasn't any different. But very few political candidates had meetings while dead women decomposed in their bomb shelters. It just isn't in good taste. Ask Dear Abby if you don't believe me. It's in her new book, Chapter 14, "Caring for Corpses." Abby is very big on spritzing them frequently with perfume.

I went back to work. Every once in a while I'd look up at the lone high window in my office and see the dusk sky begin to glow with those impossible mixtures of salmon-gold-pink-and-fuchsia that not even the best of artists can quite recreate on canvas. A quarter-moon hung exactly on the window line of moisture that would, in a couple of hours, be frost. I suppose it's a variation of self-pity, that emptiness you feel at dusk, that sense of terrible isolation. Vampires are lucky. They're just getting up about now and for them the fun is just starting. Lucky bastards.

I was hungry but not hungry. Thinking about seeing Mary sometime soon but not seeing Mary sometime soon because that probably wouldn't be a good idea for either of us. Knowing I should stop over and see Mom and Dad more often but somehow never doing it — and in a town this size, what could possibly be the excuse? Then I thought about Hastings. Had he somehow put Karen Hastings's body in the bomb shelter?

I got up and poured out the last of Jamie's pretty-damned-good coffee and then went back to my desk and wondered some more.

I was laying all this out mentally when the phone rang and a voice said, "Just stay right there." And with that she hung up.

It took me thirty seconds to play the voice back three or four times in my head. To realize who it was I'd been talking to — well, listening to. None other than the beautiful Pamela Forrest.

I thought of what Mary had said not long ago at the drugstore. It's like we were starting all over again. And it was. Or could be. Would I fall in love with Pamela all over again? Would Mary fall in love with me all over again?

I was pretty sure that vampires never had to go through stuff like this. Lucky bastards.

FIVE

It wasn't any grand entrance. In fact, she stumbled a bit coming through the door, waving a bottle of Cutty Sark. She hadn't changed in the long months since I'd seen her. A small-town Grace Kelly but without quite as much reserve. She had a pretty tart sense of humor. Tonight she was all Southern California cool, even though I assumed she'd come from Chicago. Tan suede mid-thigh jacket, white silk blouse, dark brown slacks. The golden hair was cut shorter than usual, styled in the way of TV sitcom wives and the good girls in adventure movies.

She set the scotch bottle down on my desk and said, "No waiting in line at a state liquor store, McCain. I brought it all the way from Chicago just for you."

"I don't believe it. The beautiful Pamela Forrest."

She laughed. "I take it you're still in love with me, then? I was hoping you'd be excited to see me."

I spoke carefully. "Actually, I'm not, Pamela."

But of course Pamela's ego couldn't accept anything so negative.

"Oh bullshit, McCain. You're not over me and you know it. You should see your face right this instant. You got over the surprise of seeing me. Now you look the same as you did when you used to walk me home from school in sixth grade. All moony and shy and just crazy about me."

"It must be the light in here, Pamela. But moony and shy, I'm not. The crazy part I'll admit is open to argument."

"So you're saying that if I took all my clothes off and offered myself to you, you wouldn't make love to me?"

"Well, I guess we could try it and see what happened. I guess that's about the only way we could find out for sure."

Before I knew what she was doing, she walked around my desk, shoved my chair back and pointed to my crotch. "Look at that erection, McCain. And you say you're over me. Bullshit." She went over and sat in the client chair and said, "God, I talk like a sailor these days, don't I?"

"Well, you used to be sort of prim, I guess." And she had been. This was the new but not necessarily improved Pamela.

"I wish I still was prim, McCain. You know, the good Catholic girl." Then: "I cheated on him."

"On Stu?"

"Yes. Isn't it terrible? I sound like a sailor now and I cheated on him. You know, when we were back in Catholic school I never thought I'd turn out this way. I hate myself, McCain. First, I convinced him to leave his wife and family. And then we get married and I go and cheat on him. But it was only once. But it was, unfortunately, with his best friend. But his best friend was so drunk I'm not sure he even remembers it. But I didn't think guys could, you know, *do* anything after a certain number of drinks. But you see what I mean about talking like a sailor? But I had to say all these things so you'd know why I came back here."

"Do you know how many times you started a sentence with 'but' just then?" Then I remembered again. "You ever watch *The Twilight Zone*?"

"That science fiction show on TV?"

"Yeah."

"No. It scares me too much. Why?"

"It's my favorite show. And they had a story sort of like this once."

"Like what?"

"I was talking to Mary Travers this afternoon. Wes is leaving her for another woman."

"Oh, poor Mary. She's such a good person. Poor Mary."

"That isn't the point. I'm not sure she even cares that much. She told me their marriage had never been all that good anyway."

"But she has kids."

"Two."

"Oh, poor Mary."

"My point, Pamela, is that Mary said it's like we're all starting over again — right back to where you and she and I were in high school."

"God, Wes was in love with her since fifth grade."

"Fourth."

"And then he goes and screws around on her?"

"You were in love with Stu since ninth grade and then you finally get him and you screw around on him."

"God, isn't it terrible? It's worse than terrible. It's nuts. It's pathetic. Wes waits all these years to get Mary and I wait all these years to get Stu and you wait all these years to get me and — well, I know you still want me, McCain, despite all that crap about not loving me any more. Face it. You're just too embarrassed to admit it." Giggle. "God, am I drunk." Then: "See how living in the big city has changed me?"

She was right about that. She was self-possessed now in a way you don't run into much in a town of 25,000. And I mean neither women nor men, unless they're drunk. She'd never been sweet but she'd always been soft. She wasn't really hard now but she wasn't really soft any more, either. This was a day for melancholy.

"So where're you staying?" I said.

"I thought I might spend a night or two at your place. Sneak up the back steps. I broke up a marriage here, remember? Once people start hearing that I'm back in town, it's going to be like the Salem Witch Trials."

"Why don't you stay with your folks?"

"We don't exactly get along any more, McCain. I need to warn them first with a phone call. I'm just not up to it right now. C'mon, we can get drunk on this bottle and then go to bed."

"Why couldn't you have said this three years ago when I was so damned crazy about you?"

For the first time, she seemed to understand that my feelings for her really weren't as they'd once been. I suppose I still did love her in some way. But not the old way. But not the good way.

"Because I was still in love with Stu, McCain. There wasn't anything I could do about it. God, if only I'd known how loud he snores and how bad his feet smell even after he puts foot deodorant on them. Or how he gets this real grody skin rash on his arms."

"Gee, don't you think those things are kind of superficial, Pamela? I mean, they seem like they could be solved without you boffing his best friend. I mean, did he treat you badly or anything?"

"No. He was kind and patient and loving. He really was."

"And you dumped him because he gets a skin rash?"

"Little stuff like that really bugs me, McCain. At least it did on him."

"You didn't know he got this skin rash before you married him? All the times you slept together?"

"That's the funny thing. He didn't get it till we ran off together. His doctor said it was psychosomatic. Stu would think about how he'd broken his little girl's heart and then he'd get this rash. And he wouldn't want to have sex. And then he'd get drunk. He wasn't doing so well with the law firm he joined there, either. Had a real hard time concentrating. I felt sorry for him, McCain. And I still love him in a certain way. But it all just went to hell. And really, I think it was the same for him. He had this dream about me. About how glamorous I was. But I'm not. I even bite my toenails once in a while like I did when I was a little girl. And I'm selfish and impatient and really kind of a spoiled brat for somebody who grew up in the Hills."

"Gee, no wonder I fell in love with you. All those qualities you just mentioned." I stood up, dug in my pocket, brought forth a ring of keys and tossed them to her. "You can let yourself into my apartment."

"Where're you going?"

"Business."

I plucked my topcoat from the wobbly tree rack.

"Don't I even get a kiss?" she said.

"Maybe," I said. "If you're good."

Then I was on my way.

SIX

There are two hotels and three motels in town here. I spent the next hour looking for Hastings. I had assumed he'd used a different name. But when I got to the second of the motels and described him to the desk clerk, he said, "Oh. That would be Mr. Hastings. In seventeen."

I thanked him and walked outside. The motel was on the edge of town, adjacent to the highway. Eighteen-wheelers hurtled through the night. Cars looked lonely and vulnerable in the now cold night, the wind up strong. This was the least of the motels. Rusty screen doors. Room numbers either missing or dangling from a single nail. Windows cracked and taped in front of dusty sun-parched drapes.

I knocked several times on the door of Room 17. An elderly couple gave me a skeptical, birdy eye. "I'm trying to break in here," I said. "But now I'll have to wait till you're gone."

They stared at each other. Their suspicions had been confirmed. I was indeed some kind of Martian. UFOs were in the news again and I was proof that they had landed.

They went over to a dusty green-brown Ford station wagon the color of baby poop and pulled away.

I didn't break in. Instead I took my penlight and went over to the cars parked near the room. The licenses were mostly from the Midwest, Minnesota and Wisconsin particularly. None from Illinois.

I went back to the registration desk.

"How many nights did Mr. Hastings pay for?"

The worn man with the worn cardigan sweater and the worn blue eyes said, "I'm not sure I should be tellin' things like that."

I showed him my license. *The Real McCoys* was on in the background.

"Oh, you're the fella that works for that judge. She's sure an owly one. I got four parking tickets and forgot to pay 'em and the way she treated me you'd'a thought I just killed a couple of nuns."

I laughed. "That's the Judge."

"Way I hear it she's still mad because the Sykes family bought this town out from under her."

"That's the way I hear it, too."

" 'Course I don't have no time for the Sykes family, neither. At least she's kinda classy. Way she dresses and all. And that car she drives. What's it called?"

"A Bentley."

"That's some car. The Sykeses, though, they're just a bunch of hillbillies." He referenced his small black-and-white TV set with a nod of his narrow, angular head. "Like old Walter Brennan on the TV."

"I need to know about Hastings."

"Well, you work for the Judge, too, don'tcha?"

"Yes."

"Well, I guess it'd be all right. He registered for three nights."

"When'd he roll in?"

"Two nights ago. About this time."

"So this would be his last night?"

"Yep. Guess so."

"How about you call me when he comes in tonight? I probably won't be there but a woman will answer. You can leave the message with her."

"All right." Then: "Ain't you gonna bribe me? I could use a couple bucks."

"That's only in movies."

"Really? I figured people like you bribed people like me all the time."

I dug in my pocket. I had a crumpled dollar and a quarter. "This'll get you a burger and a pack of smokes. And you'll have some change left over."

"Hey," he said, sounding young and vital suddenly. "That's all right. A buck and a quarter." He quickly scooped up the money and shoved it in his pants, watching me suspiciously as he did so, as if I might try and take it back.

As I was walking out the door, he said, "You think the Russians are gonna run that blockade ole Kennedy set up?"

"I sure hope not."

"Scares the hell out of me," he said. "Scares the hell out of me."

Jim Gilliam turned out to be a very slick public relations man. The Brooks Brothers suit, the filter cigarettes, black horn-rimmed glasses, the smooth empty patter. Shrewd eyes that approved of very little they saw.

He stood in the doorway of the Murdoch mansion, blocking my entrance.

"I wish I could let you in but Mr. Murdoch is still in the meeting."

"That's one long meeting."

"Well, that's how political campaigns are, Mr. McCain. Night and day. Day and night."

"Cole Porter."

"Pardon me?"

" 'Night and day. Day and night.' That's a Cole Porter song."

"Oh, right," he said. "The song. Very good, Mr. McCain. You should go on a game show."

I blurted her name as soon as I saw her crossing from one part of the huge house to the other. "Deirdre!"

She turned, peered into the darkness of the vestibule, and then came walking toward me. "Is that you, Sam?"

"Yep. But Jim here won't let me in."

"What's that supposed to mean — he won't let you in? He'll let you in if I tell him to. And I'm telling him to right now."

She looked irritated and Gilliam looked irritated. Just then a big gray tomcat went walking by. He looked irritated, too, come to think of it.

"He happens to be a friend of mine, Jim."

"I'm just trying to protect your Dad."

"Sam's *helping* my Dad, Jim."

"But the meeting —"

"It's not a political meeting. It's just his three best friends is all."

I didn't know how much Gilliam knew — if anything — about dead girls in bomb shelters or four men who chipped in to support the same mistress but I could see that he knew something. Or knew at the very least that his candidate had some kind of terrible personal problem. Now he didn't look irritated. He looked nervous. Extremely.

Deirdre seemed unaware of any tension. She said, "C'mon in, Sam. You can meet Mom. We were just drinking some hot cocoa in the family room."

Gilliam stepped aside. "I'm just trying to do my job, Sam. Nothing personal."

"I know." And I did. I'd been put in the same position many times. Screening people is not a way to make friends.

I tapped him on the elbow to show no hard feelings.

"God," she said, as she led me to the family room. "This campaign is terrible. It's like we're all prisoners. We have to watch everything we do and say. Even where we go and who we see. I'm pretty sure Dad's going to win. And I'm pretty sure things'll be even worse in the governor's mansion."

But the governor's mansion was getting lost in the midst of scandal. You could barely see it from here. And each hour it grew fainter and fainter.

"Mom, this is Sam McCain."

The family room was painted white with bold colorful paintings on the wall and blonde Swedish furniture gathered around the twenty-seven inch TV console. A magazine advertisement.

"It's very nice to meet you, Sam. My husband and Deirdre both say very nice things about you."

"It's all that money I pay them."

Deirdre nudged me in the ribs. "I told you he was a wise-guy, Mom."

"Would you care for some hot cocoa?" Mom said. "I was just going out to the kitchen to get some more for myself." She slid a rather short, wide hand at me. "My name's Irene, by the way."

"Nice to meet you, Irene." In her tan slacks and brown turtleneck sweater and dark silken hair cut short, her body gave the impression of strength and activity. Dressed for action. She was a big woman but it appeared not to be fat, just the shape of her natural body.

"Would you like some cocoa, Sam?" Deirdre said.

"Sure."

"I'll go help Mom, then. We'll be right back."

"Thanks. Cocoa sounds good."

As soon as they'd left the room, I hurried through the house, looking for the den where I'd talked earlier in the day with Ross Murdoch.

I kept a lookout for Gilliam. He had every right to ask me why I was walking alone through the house. Especially if he happened to catch me with my ear pressed to the door of the den.

But I didn't see him. And I found the den with no trouble. A low rumble of male voices pressed against the other side of the door but no intelligible words escaped.

His three best friends, Deirdre had said. The men who had to make a damned quick decision. The men who had reputations and minor fortunes to lose once this thing got out. The men who would be the most likely suspects of all when Cliffie finally came into possession of the body. And Ross Murdoch would be at the head of that suspect list.

I knocked softly, one of those two-knuckle jobs.

I wasn't sure anybody'd heard me. They kept right on talking. And then, in delayed response, the low male rumble stopped entirely. Silence. Followed by footsteps.

Ross Murdoch opened the door and said, "Damn."

"Same to you."

"I didn't mean it that way, Sam. It's just so damned — confusing."

I peered into the den. Three men sat in chairs collected around his huge desk. They all half-turned to see what annoying little bastard had interrupted their meeting. I recognized all of them. Community leaders, as they were always referred to in the local newspaper.

"I guess you got here just in time," Murdoch said. "We were about to take a vote."

"I don't want him in here," said prissy Peter Carlson.

"Neither do I," said grumpy Gavin Wheeler.

"Isn't he that asshole private eye?" said mean Mike Hardin.

"I guess you may as well come in," Murdoch said.

"Yeah, sounds like they're really looking forward to me joining in the fun."

He laughed wearily. "They're just afraid you'll back me up and try to talk them out of it."

"Talk them out of what?"

He sighed deeply. "They want to take the body out of the bomb shelter and throw it in the river."

"Say," I said. "That's a really good idea. Juries love to hear little tidbits like that. That way they don't have to spend a lot of time convicting you. They can probably be out of the jury room in under ten minutes."

Murdoch laughed.

Mean Mike Hardin said, "See, I told you he was an asshole."

SEVEN

Sinclair Lewis had written, and not as un-charitably as memory has it, of their fathers and grandfathers. I know stuff like this because at the U of Iowa I took my major in English and my minor in pre-law.

Lewis called them boosters, by which he meant that they promoted themselves, their communities and their country with the relentless fervor of marchers in a Fourth of July parade. They believed, and took as their secular religion, a former president's statement that "The business of America is business."

Fine and dandy. Not anything wrong with that. The trouble was that they defined themselves, their communities and their country in pretty restrictive ways. You needed to be the right color, the right religion and the right political philosophy to be their friends and to share in their success.

In this case, the four men sitting in Ross

Murdoch's den had inherited modest wealth from their fathers and had doubled or tripled that wealth all by themselves. They were bright and savvy men. They had served in the big war or in the Korean war, one of them in both, so you sure couldn't question their very admirable patriotism. Two of them had their own airplanes; one of them ran a Canadian resort as an escape and a side business; and one of them wanted very much to be governor. What always surprised me was their bitterness and anger, which they rarely expressed when they were sober. But I'd been Judge Whitney's uneasy and self-conscious guest at the country club a few nights and had stood at the bar with men very much like these. In their cups, they sounded as if they were the most oppressed minority in the country. Their world was coming apart. The colored athletes at the U of Iowa were sleeping with respectable white girls. The goddamn Japs were starting to flood the free markets with low-priced trash. The State Department wanted American farmers to share all their agricultural secrets with these little countries that would turn around and undercut American crop prices. Rock-and-roll was mostly queers and horny Negroes who belonged in prison just on general principles. Edward R. Murrow, who'd always been a troublemaker, had taken up the cause of Mexican farm workers and so now the big farmers had to worry about a federal agent hiding behind every tree. And, despite all the warnings from Billy Graham and Norman Vincent Peale, you had a Catholic in the White House who was probably on the phone to the Pope three times a day.

Part of their boozy unhappiness had struck me as sheer age. You saw some of it in the blue collar taverns where I drank and belonged. I wasn't idealizing them. They had plenty of their own prejudices and rages. But then it didn't sound as if all the world was conspiring to overthrow them. They were men lamenting all the girls they should've screwed — *God, if I'd only known then what I know now* — and usually imaginary chances they'd had to invest in this or that scheme to become millionaires overnight much as Jackie Gleason tried to become every Saturday night as "Ralph Kramden," the working-class fool with a heart of embarrassing but endearing dreams. They wanted to be young and virile again; they were worried their kids were going to be cut in the next bunch of layoffs at the plant because their seniority was so low; they were melancholy that as much as they loved their wives and their wives loved them there just wasn't that spark there any more, *You shoulda seen her when she was nineteen, McCain, at the swimming pool in Jackson Park. She'd walk out into the sunlight and the guys would just cream their jeans right there. Right on the spot. Cream their jeans. And I was one of 'em. And she picked me. Me!*

But generally there wasn't the rage, the rancor I found in the booster class. The workers had simpler and thus less frustrating hopes — they just wanted their kids to do better than they did and to be safe and to not get in any trouble with the law or nothing like that. But the country club men — they had dreamed far larger dreams and saw evidence everywhere that it was all going away for them.

"So you're suggesting what exactly?" said Mike Hardin. Third string guard at a small liberal arts college in New Hampshire. His law office covered with framed photos of himself in his football days. He was the preferred lawyer of the wealthy in this part of the state. And for good reason. He was smart and wily and commanded a courtroom with an easy grace I could only envy.

"Mike. You're a lawyer. Listen to what you're saying." I said this after fifteen minutes of listening to several nit-wit alternatives to just calling Cliffie.

"Don't give me any lectures, McCain. You're nobody, I mean in case you hadn't noticed." He had one of those taut, angular faces that reflected perfectly the mood of the moment.

"For God's sake, Mike," Ross Murdoch said. "You're nobody and I'm nobody — we're all nobody."

"I'd forgotten how humble you are, Ross," Hardin said. "But I guess that's why you've always been morally superior to the rest of us."

"Shut the hell up, Mike," Gavin Wheeler said. Wheeler was in his forties, looked sixty. He was always dressed in a three-piece suit, the assumption being, I guess, that the vest hid his enormous belly. He was bald and had the largest hands I'd ever seen. He'd been a wrestler at the U of Iowa and a damned good one. He'd seen the future as soon as he'd come back from the big war. He and a rich cousin had started four TV stations. They now had ten stations here and in Missouri and were very, very rich. "We acted like a bunch of stupid bastards when we agreed to bring her out here. I still can't believe we did it. But we did and now she's downstairs — dead. Listening to McCain here — we've been kidding ourselves. We've made things a lot worse for ourselves already. We've waited a whole day to call the law. But I'm throwing in with McCain. I say let's call Cliffie now and salvage what we can of it."

Peter Carlson had a yacht on the Mississippi, a twin-engine Bonanza at the Cedar Rapids airport, and a Hugh Hefner pad in Chicago. He divided his time between running his stock brokerage and gossiping. You couldn't pass him on the street without him stopping you to tell you something nasty about somebody you knew. And if he didn't have gossip, he always had his scorn. He had one of those smug, imperious temperaments that intimidated you through its malice.

"I just want to say one thing," Carlson said. He was a slim, short, preppy-looking man who always managed to work in the fact that he'd graduated from Yale. That is, if you'd managed to miss the enormous Yale class ring on his finger. If the Yale Alumni Association had recommended Yale tattoos, I'm sure he'd have one on his forehead. "Think of our wives, think of our kids, think of our parents when this hits the newspapers and the TV sets. Our lives are over. No matter who killed her and put her down in that bomb shelter. Our lives are over no matter how it turns out. We'll always be the four civic leaders who set up a woman — let's face it, a very high-priced whore — in an apartment so we wouldn't have to travel very far when we wanted a little nookie on the side. Are you ready to face that?"

Mike Hardin half-leaped from his chair and started pacing. "Face it. We're screwed either way we go." He made huge frustrated fists of his hands. He wanted to rip something apart. If I'd been in his situation, I'd have reacted the same way. He walked over to the window and looked outside. Nobody talked. A grandfather clock in the corner made the only sound.

"The longer you wait, the worse it'll be," I said. "And even if you try to hide the body, it'll be found and you'll still have to face all the same problems."

"I'm willing to call Cliffie right now." Ross Murdoch held an unlit briar pipe. A pacifier for older tots. "And I'm going to be the number one suspect." He sighed again. "And it's going to be the end of my political career."

He'd obviously been thinking realistically about everything in the hours I'd been away.

"Your career is finished, Ross," I said. "But all four of you'll be suspects."

"Us?" snapped Peter Carlson. "It's not our bomb shelter. It's Ross's. We don't live here."

"No, but you were one-fourth of the deal."

"Does he have to be here, Ross?" Carlson said. "He's some two-bit lawyer. He doesn't know jack shit."

"Well, *I'm* not a two-bit lawyer and I say he's right on the money," Hardin said. "Hell, yes, we're all going to be suspects. The workers in and out all day. Doors opened wide. I imagine there were times when nobody in the family was home when the bomb shelter was being worked on. Anybody could've slipped in. Any one of us. She probably weighed a little over a hundred pounds. She wouldn't be hard to move in if you got in right after the workers were done for the day and the family was gone. *Were* you all gone yesterday, Ross?"

"I was in Iowa City. I'll have to check with my wife and daughter. The maid usually leaves around four. She leaves the dinner for us in the stove. We like to eat early, around five."

"There you go. You see what I mean?" Hardin said. "This house is big enough that people on the second floor wouldn't hear anybody if they snuck into the basement and were quiet about it."

"Cliffie isn't that smart," Gavin Wheeler said.

"Cliffie won't have to be smart," Murdoch said. "I know enough people in the capital that I can insist on the state boys getting involved. I want to find out what the hell happened."

Gavin Wheeler said, "My own TV stations'll cover this. I'll be sittin' at home watchin' my own TV station treat me like a common criminal. Damned good thing it's privately held. Stockholders'd kick my ass out for sure."

"We're all going to have those problems," Murdoch said. "People'll be shocked when they hear this. And then they'll start laughing. And they'll laugh at us the rest of our lives. It'll be like when Carmichael took bankruptcy."

Andy Carmichael had owned twenty-some mom and pop grocery stores throughout the state. He wasn't afraid of the huge supermarkets that had just reached the outlying Midwest. He said that people in our kind of towns would resist them. Would hate the size. Would hate the impersonal service. Would hate all the hoopla that always goes along with places like that. Two supermarkets came into town in 1950 and by 1952 all of Carmichael's stores were out of business and he'd gone bankrupt. He took to walking with his head down so he wouldn't have to acknowledge anyone on the street. He took to staying home for days, sometimes weeks at a time. He took to solitary and severe drinking. And then one night he took to putting a .45 in his mouth and pulling the trigger. Just once is all it takes. It wasn't Jews, Negroes, homosexuals, or even Catholics — despite the name he was a virulent anti-Papist Protestant — that had done him in. It was capitalism in its simplest and most ruthless form.

Murdoch set his pipe on the desk, walked around so he could face everybody and said, "I'm going to call Cliffie. Sam, you shouldn't be here. That'll make things look bad for you and bad for us. I'm going to tell one lie that I want you all to agree with. That I didn't discover the body until just before dinner. That way it won't look as if we even considered covering all this up. I found the body, called you gentlemen over, and we all arranged to be here when the law arrived. Is that all right?"

"I won't swear to it under oath," I said. "In fact, I think it's a very bad idea. Lies never work in investigations like these."

Murdoch shook his head. "I'm going to take the chance."

"That's up to you, Ross."

I nodded to the four of them. "Good luck."

I had almost closed the door — hoping I wouldn't hear any disparaging whispers about myself — when Peter Carlson, obviously wanting me to hear it, said, "What a nickel-dimer he is. I don't want him around any more, Ross, and I mean it."

All the way out to my car I wondered which was more insulting, nickel-dimer or asshole. I am frequently involved in such philosophical debates.

I was so lost in asshole versus nickel-dimer that I didn't even see her until I opened the door and got in the car. She sat smoking a cigarette in the passenger seat.

Her hair was in a ponytail now and she wore a crew neck sweater, white shirt and jeans. She looked like a high school girl. "Hope you don't mind."

"Not at all."

"God, I love making out in cars, don't

you? And I don't mean that as an invitation."

"Yeah, I do."

"And then smoking afterward. And drawing your initials in the steam on the window. And pretending that nobody can ever hurt you as long as you never leave the car. And as long as the night never ends."

She was bringing back a lot of memories and for a long wonderful moment I rode on the crest of them, surfer style. But then I began wondering what she was doing out here.

She spoke before I could ask her.

"I just had to get away from my mom for a while."

"I thought you got along."

"We do. But — today's been a real strain on her."

"I'm sorry to hear that."

She said, "She's been eating Miltowns all day."

"Still the tranquilizer of choice."

"She's terrified and so am I."

"Of what?"

"Oh, please, Sam. Something terrible's going on, isn't it? Dad won't let anybody go in the basement and if you even go near it, he explodes. He's usually very calm.

Then his three so-called 'friends' have this secret meeting in the den."

"Why 'so-called'?"

"Well, both Hardin and Carlson have tried to put the make on me ever since I was fourteen. Hardin even got me drunk one night at this New Year's Eve party and really felt me up."

"Our esteemed counselor?"

"Our esteemed counselor."

"Anything else I should know about?"

She angled herself over so that she could lay back against the window. "I love the feeling of a cold car window on your skin. If I had a blanket I could probably go to sleep right here."

"It's my company. I have that effect on people. I once put an entire stadium asleep by telling them my life story. And I only got up to age two before they all nodded off."

She smiled. "I'll bet a lot of girls have told you how cute you are."

"I'll bet a lot of guys have told you how beautiful *you* are."

" 'Pretty,' I'll go along with. Beautiful — no."

"You never did finish telling me about our esteemed counselor Hardin."

"I know. I just feel kind of funny — you

know. Talking about private family things."

I didn't want to push her. Make her any more suspicious about what was going on all around her. I just said, "Well — and please don't tell anybody else this — the same thing happened to me."

"What same thing?"

"With Hardin. He got *me* drunk one night and felt *me* up, too. But then he dropped me when he found out I couldn't mambo."

She laughed. "You must've been crushed."

"Well, not really. His breath is pretty bad."

She leaned over and kissed me. "You really are an idiot, you know."

"So give me some dirt on Hardin. He's a competitor of mine in a way. I just enjoy hearing things about competitors."

She shrugged and then leaned back against the window.

"Well, it's not anything hot or sexy. It's just this housing development in Des Moines. Wheeler and Dad went ahead and invested in it and made a lot of money. They didn't invite Hardin or Carlson in. Hardin and Dad actually got into a fist fight in the den over it. Hardin was adamant about it for months. He seems to believe that they made some kind of agreement to always act as a group. And that any time there's an investment opportunity, they should all be told about it. You know, have the right to turn it down at least."

"So he gets along with Wheeler?"

"Oh, God," she said and put her head back against the seat. "I really shouldn't say this. But I had two drinks and that always turns me into a snitch. You know how in the big war they always said 'Loose lips sink ships'?"

"There were posters everywhere that said that."

"Well, after two or three drinks, I sink a lot of ships."

"Meaning?"

She couldn't decide if she wanted to sink any more ships. While she was deciding, I saw a car pull up at the distant entrance to the place and cut its lights. I recognized the car immediately. A white and blue 1955 Chevrolet. The car that changed automobile styles around the world. Probably my all-time favorite design. There were still a number of them around. But I had the feeling I knew whose car it was.

"My father once accused Wheeler of

cheating him in a land deal. They patched things up but they've never been very close since. I think the only reason they see each other at all is because they have so many investments together." She tamped out another cigarette. "So now it's your turn."

"My turn?"

"You have to tell me what's going on with my father. And why you keep looking in your rearview mirror."

"There's a car parked near the entrance to your drive."

"A burglar?" she said lightly.

"A reporter."

"Not the intrepid Don Arbogast."

I laughed. "Yes, indeed. The intrepid Don Arbogast, the man who gave narcolepsy a bad name."

Don was, depending on whom you believed, in his seventies or eighties. It was believed that he had something naughty on his employer. How else could he keep his job? He hobbled around on a walker half the time. And the other half — as when he was covering trials — he sat in the back and snored. He was a decent guy and had once been a first-rate reporter. These days he'd get lucky once in a while and stumble into a story that really mattered.

"Well, at least we don't have to worry

about him coming up here and bothering us. He can't walk that far."

"I think I'll check him out," I said.

"Hey," she said. "You're supposed to tell me what's going on with my father."

"C'mon now, I need to talk to Arbogast before he leaves."

"Leaves? He's probably asleep."

And he probably was.

I leaned across her and opened the door. "I need to hurry."

"This isn't fair." She was still keeping the tone light, a kind of mock petulance. But her eyes were anxious. She rightly suspected that something was badly wrong.

She got out of the Ford and said, "I hope I'll see you tomorrow. By then maybe I'll know what's going on around here."

I drove away.

The intrepid Don Arbogast was just getting out of his nifty mobile when I pulled up alongside him on the road in front of the Murdoch place.

I always felt sorry for him. Couldn't help it. His wife had died ten years ago, his kids were grown and dispersed throughout the galaxy, and he had no life but his reporting job. The paper had two young reporters to do the heavy work. The publisher just sort of let Don do whatever he wanted to.

I wished he hadn't dyed his hair black. I wished he didn't wear drape-style sports coats of the kind most often seen on Elvis Presley. I wished he didn't wear bow ties, pinkie rings and a snap-brim fedora. He didn't seem to understand that all this was lost in the old-man shuffle and the old-man drool.

I rolled down my window and said, "Kinda nippy tonight, Don."

"Yeah, but I dig cold weather."

Which was another thing. He used a lot of "cool" slang. Oh, Don Don Don.

"You having engine trouble?" I said, nodding to that enviably cherry vehicle of his.

"Huh?" He cupped his hand to his ear like a hearing horn.

"YOU HAVING ENGINE TROUBLE?" I guess I forgot to mention the hard-of-hearing thing.

"No, man, I'm just checkin' out a tip."

"What kind of tip?" My stomach started to feel funny, tense and vaguely sick.

"Somebody called and said there was a dead body in the Murdoch place. He's runnin' for senator, you know."

"Governor, actually."

"Huh?" Again with the hand to the ear.

100

I decided to let this one pass. "You remember who called you with the tip, Don?"

This one he heard. His face broke into a smile that made him look twenty years younger. "You think I'd fink on a source of mine?" And then those old sad-dog brown eyes got a lot brighter. He was like a boxer who is flat on his back at the count of nine but who suddenly springs to his feet and starts throwing killer punches. That was why you couldn't ever dismiss him. Just when you thought he could never put a story together, he'd give you a tale that would rock you. "And by the way, McCain, what're you doing out here?"

"Just visiting Deirdre."

"She's got some caboose on her, don't she?"

"She sure does." And she did.

"The wife, she had a caboose like that. Kept it, too, right up to the end."

I smiled. "She was a good woman, Don." A little woman, quick and attractive, her well-known sorrow being that she'd never been able to have kids. Out of a Hamlin Garland or Willa Cather story, in her way.

I thought of driving back to the house and warning them about Don. But what was the point? Cliffie would be out here soon enough and Don would have his story. What I was more interested in was who had called him and tipped him.

And then I had reason to realize all over again how you could underestimate this old guy. He leaned back through his car window and brought forth a pair of binoculars. High-powered ones from the looks of them. He scanned the driveway. "That's interesting."

"What is?"

"Just a sec."

Our idling motors made a good deal of noise and my headlights speared through gathering ground fog.

"Looks like Hardin, Wheeler, and Carlson. Their cars, I mean. Somethin' must be up. That tip was a good one."

"Probably just having a business meeting of some kind."

"Guess I'll drive up there and see if they'll talk to me."

"Well, good luck, Don."

"Bet them boys are gonna be surprised to see me."

I sure couldn't argue with him about that one.

EIGHT

I found a phone booth downtown and called the motel where Hastings was staying. A woman was on the desk now. She told me he hadn't come back yet, that she'd just checked the rooms — they'd had trouble with teenagers trying to sneak into vacant rooms — and there was no sign of him. She said that her father, the guy I'd bribed with money enough for a burger and a pack of smokes with some change left over, had given her instructions to call me right away when she saw him.

I called Kenny Thibodeau, Pornographer and unofficial Private Eye.

"Hey McCain, how they hangin'?"

"Y'know, Kenny, you really should quit saying that to everybody who calls."

"I don't say it to chicks."

"Yeah, but I mean what if the Pope or somebody called you?"

"Why would the Pope call me?"

"I'm just saying for instance the Pope."

"I'd say, Hey, Padre, how they hangin'?"

I laughed. "I don't think you've changed much since we were in fifth grade."

"Well, I didn't know how to write dirty paperbacks back then."

"I guess that's a good point. So what did you dredge up for me from all these mysterious sources of yours?"

"Hardin's broke."

"Hardin? He's one of the wealthiest lawyers in the state."

"California cleaned him out."

"What happened in California?"

As I leaned against the inside of the booth, I saw a group of people coming through the doors of the Presbyterian church across the street. They held long white candles that burned in golden nimbuses. There were maybe forty of them in a long line of pairs. A cross-section of folks, white collar and blue collar alike. Rich and poor. They walked down the street saying the Lord's Prayer. Not hard to figure out the occasion. They were praying to whatever gods there be that this planet and its people would not be subjected to what Hiroshima and Nagasaki had had to endure. And were still enduring. Today's bombs were many times more powerful than those had been.

"Hey, McCain, you still there?"

"Hey, Kenny, how they hangin'?"

"Very funny."

"I got distracted. So tell me about California."

The long line reached the end of the block and turned toward the business section. There would be a rally tonight where people from all four churches would meet in the town square to pray and sing hymns. According to Walter Cronkite, this was going on all over the country. Khrushchev had yet to respond in any fashion to the naval blockade.

"Condos. Sank about everything he had in condos with his brother-in-law out there. I guess they both got dazzled when this old movie star — Rex Thomas, you remember him, right after the war? — anyway this Thomas guy was building these condominiums on the ocean front. First thing Hardin did was ask for safety of the land to be evaluated. You sink all this money into building condos and they tumble into the ocean some night, you got some real problems.

"Anyway, the guy Hardin hires — some guy this LA lawyer recommended — he says you'd have to be crazy to build where Rex Thomas wants to. So Hardin and his brother-in-law are all ready to pull out but Thomas convinces them to get a second opinion."

"I think I can see this one coming."

"So they get this guy they meet who's checking out the land for some other investors and Hardin gets along with him — naturally the guy is impressive — and so Hardin says let's let this guy check out the land. If he says it's all right —"

"Rex Thomas knows the guy. Told him to pretend to be checking out the land for these other mysterious investors."

"Then you can write the rest of this yourself, man. Hardin and his brother-in-law give Rex Thomas practically everything they've got. The condos get built."

"And tumble into the ocean?"

"Not yet. It's going to happen. But it hasn't happened yet."

"So how did Hardin lose his money?"

"What Thomas — who is now in Europe somewhere marrying this countess and making the same kind of swashbucklers he used to make in Hollywood — what Thomas did was cheapjack the shit out of the construction. They're like a thousand times shoddier than regular housing developments. I mean, the toilets don't flush, the doors fall off, the air conditioning sounds like a B-52 when you start it up. Like that."

"So Thomas cheapjacked the work and pocketed the difference."

"And that difference may be as much as two hundred thousand dollars."

"They can't sue?"

"Chapter Thirteen. Thomas set up his own corporation and ran everything through there. Soon as the first residents moved in, he declares Chapter Thirteen and skies over to Europe to marry this countess chick."

" 'Skies'?"

"Yeah. I read that in *Variety* the other day."

"So he's broke."

"Just about. But I'm not sure what any of this would have to do with whatever's going on that you won't tell me about."

"I don't either. I'll have to run it through my giant brain several times before I can figure it out."

"Well, that's all I've got."

"Thanks, Kenny."

"You owe me a meal."

"You like drive-up windows?"

"A real meal, McCain. A real meal."

After I'd hung up, I stood outside the phone booth in the chill night, smoking my

Lucky and listening to the singing of the group that had just left the church. It was hopeful and despairing at the same time, that trapeze flight of our existence.

I was on the right side of town to check out Hastings's motel so I decided to break a few laws tonight, pick his lock and peek inside. On the way over, I thought of the four grim men sitting in Ross Murdoch's den. Murdoch would pick up the phone and call Cliffie, and Murdoch's life in a very real sense would end. As would the lives of the other three men. All the people who'd envied them, all the people they'd pushed around to get their way, all the home-grown moralists would become an angry Greek chorus. From the pulpit, though their names would not be used, they would be denounced as libertines and used as examples of our corrupt age; and in the taverns they would be denounced as laughing-stocks and used as examples of how rich guys had all the advantages when it came to women.

I passed a shiny new motel with late model shark-finned cars in all the parking lots and a general air of prosperity in the landscaping, the signage and the clean, inviting, brightly lit front office.

I parked half a block from Hastings's motel. No air of prosperity here. A kind of prairie grimness: low-echelon traveling salesmen; beer tavern romeos and romeoettes trying to blot out the burden of spouses and kids waiting so hungrily for them at home; and sad itinerant families with too many kids and never enough money, traveling to where some magazine told them were good-paying jobs that always seemed to be have just been filled when they arrived. Then back into their rusty beaten old trucks and on to the highway again, satisfied to settle for minimum wage and three squares a day — if they can only find it.

Country music twang; sitcom robot laughter; slap and tickle, thrust and groan — all the familiar sounds of motel life behind those heavy dusty faded curtains and loose doors a ten-year-old could open if you gave him a few minutes.

I used my old Cub Scout pocket knife. Best eighty-nine cents I'd ever spent. I was inside in less than thirty seconds.

I used a penlight to look around. There was a briefcase that didn't reveal a lot besides his taste in reading. Three western paperbacks by Luke Short. At least he had good taste in frontier stories.

I found what I wanted in a manila envelope. I sat down in a chair and lighted a cigarette and started looking through all the clippings. In case he decided to burst through the door, I put my .38 in my lap.

There was, it seemed, a magic act known as "The Majestic Magic-ans." Judging by the clippings, they played every kind of venue there was, from the seamier lounges in Vegas to VFW halls in Beloit, Wisconsin. Most of the clippings weren't reviews, just notices that "The Majestic Magic-ans" were about to or had appeared there.

There were two reviews and both of them were moderately favorable as to the magic part of the show but almost lascivious when it came to the male reviewer discussing the "beautiful assistant Shandra." She sure as hell was beautiful, especially half-naked in her Magic-ans costume. The only time I'd seen her she was dead back there in the bomb shelter.

The magician was a plucky little guy in a cheap tux and a top hat. According to the reviews his name was Michael Reeves and Shandra was his sister. I knew him, of course, as Hastings the bounty hunter. Seeing them together in the newspaper photos I saw, for the first time, a family resemblance. General shape of head; the shape of the eyes. On her the physical details were beautiful; on him they were undefined, unfinished somehow, not long enough in the kiln perhaps, the way a little kid's face is unfinished.

In the back of the envelope were several glossies of various luminaries standing with the Magic-ans. They ran to TV stars who no longer had shows to sports stars who didn't get in the game as much as they used to. The men always managed to have a possessive arm slung around Shandra's neck. One of them — and this made me laugh out loud — was quite obviously peering down her very low-cut gown. All the glossies were scribbled with all the usual show-biz bullshit accolades. "Greatest magic act I've ever seen!" "To two dear friends!" I wished just one of them would have been honest and said, "I'd pay a million bucks to get into your knickers, Shandra!" You know, break the monotony of all the hype and get to the real subject at hand.

I had to take a leak and so I did. And while I was standing there at the john I smelled it. There's no other odor like it.

I got done, zipped up, washed my hands in the rusty sink, turned around and faced the narrow closet door. He probably hadn't taken to smelling too bad when the owner's daughter made a quick sweep of the room earlier. And there would have been no reason for her to look in the closet.

I took a deep breath and opened the closet door and damned if he didn't fall straight out at me the way closeted corpses always did in "Abbott and Costello" movies.

I pushed him back inside quickly. Propping up corpses is way down on my list of things that give me pleasure, right next to emptying bedpans and listening to Paul Harvey.

But I still had to hold him up with one hand while I used my penlight to find the wound that had killed him. Didn't take long. Somebody had used something heavy to smash in the back left side of his head. Wouldn't take all that much.

I had to slam the door shut quick so he wouldn't fall out again. I heard his forehead bounce off the inside of the door. If he hadn't been dead, he sure was now.

Then I went to the phone and dialed the police station. The dispatcher, who was a good guy, told me all about the body in the bomb shelter and said that every cop on the shift was out there except for Lonesome Bob Tehearn who was, by any reckoning, in the fates-worse-than-death category when you wanted help with a murder investigation. But I needed somebody to come out here, listen to my story, and then take over.

"Well, I'll see if I can find him. You know, Lonesome Bob takes an awful lot of naps," the dispatcher said, "and sometimes he sleeps right through my calls."

"Well, if you can wake him up, please send him over here."

"I'll do what I can, McCain. But it may take a little while. Especially if he's at the park. He's got this little nook there where he really sacks out. I like it better when he just pulls into an alley downtown. The teenagers usually spot him and start throwing stuff at his car. That way he don't sleep so long."

Lonesome Bob Tehearn was Cliffie's first cousin, in case you're wondering how he'd lasted so long on the force.

Lonesome Bob arrived thirty-five minutes later. He was a tall, lanky hound dog of a man with stooped shoulders and a grin he grinned frequently and seemingly for no reason at all. He was also the proud

113

owner of a truckload of cheap after-shave. It was so strong that if you ever stood downwind of it, tears would start streaming down your cheeks.

He got the name "Lonesome Bob" in the days after World War II when he found himself being asked to be the best man at the wedding of the girl he'd been engaged to all the time he was overseas. The groom had formerly been Bob's best friend, a 4-F'er on account of an old knee injury. Or so he said, his uncle on the draft board notwithstanding.

For reasons unfathomable to most of our species, Lonesome Bob accepted, thus making everybody at the wedding extremely nervous as they waited for him to pull out a gun and kill the bride and groom. But no such thing happened.

Lonesome Bob had never married. He lived in a small cabin a mile out of town, the exterior walls being decorated with license plates from all over the world. Most folks couldn't stand to go inside Lonesome Bob's cabin because of all the squirrel meat he fried and ate. Lonesome Bob liked to say that eating squirrel took care of two of his passions — hunting and eating.

People tell me that squirrel meat tastes pretty good but I've never been able to get close enough to it to find out. The stench'll make blood start firing from your ears.

While Lonesome Bob went in and looked at Hastings, or whatever his real name was, I called my apartment to see how the beautiful Pamela Forrest was doing.

Doing pretty well, I thought the instant she said hello. She was drunk and giggly. I'd gotten over being mad at her. She hadn't humiliated me all those years; *I* had humiliated me all those years. Not her problem that I was foolish enough to hang on to the bumper while her car dragged me over burning coals and broken glass. I was trying to be rational and reasonable about all those heartbroken years I'd spent pursuing her because I'd decided that sleeping with her tonight sounded pretty damned good. Bygones be bygones and all that. At least until dawn.

"Hey! Sam baby!"

Sam baby? "You sound like you're in a pretty good mood."

"Best mood I've been in a long time." Then she hiccoughed. "God, am I bombed."

"Gee, really. I hadn't noticed."

"You're so — what's the word?"

"Sarcastic?"

"Yeah. Right. Sarcastic."

"Well, I was worrying you might be depressed or something was why I called. But you seem to be doing all right."

Then she got coy, playful. I'd never heard her be coy and playful before. I actually hated coy and playful. "Wait'll you get here, Sam baby. You're gonna be surprised." And before I could say anything: "And you know what else, Sam baby?"

"Y'got me." Talking to drunks is so much fun.

"Every one of your cats loves me."

"That's nice."

"They fight over who gets to sit in my lap." Hiccough.

"Y'know, you might think of drinking a little coffee. There's some instant in the cupboard."

"Boy, am I drunk."

"Did you hear what I said?"

"Said about what?"

"Said about instant coffee in the cupboard."

"When did you say that? And anyway, I hate instant coffee."

I couldn't take any more. "I'll see you in a while."

"Toodles, Sam baby." And then she gig-

116

gled and dropped the receiver.

I walked to the back of the room. Lonesome Bob had Hastings laid out on the floor.

"How's it going?" I said.

"He's dead."

"I know he's dead. I mean, did you find anything useful?"

He'd been haunched down next to the corpse, playing the beam of a silver flashlight over the body. When he stood up, his knees cracked. "All that scientific stuff. I don't get it at all. I leave that to Cliff. About all I could tell you about this guy was that somebody smashed his head in."

Lonesome Bob and the beautiful Pamela Forrest could have a very interesting conversation right about now. But I was just bitter because poor Lonesome Bob here was something of a dope and the beautiful Pamela Forrest was going to cheat me out of a night of sex by being unconscious by the time I got back to my apartment.

"Say," said Lonesome Bob, "I just thought of something."

"What's that?"

"You didn't kill this fella, did you?"

"No; no, I didn't, Lonesome Bob."

He narrowed his hound dog eyes and

said, "Don't kid me now, McCain. Did you kill this fella?"

"I didn't kill him, Lonesome Bob. He was dead before I got here."

He studied me some and said, "That's why I don't need that scientific crap. I just look people right in the eye and I can tell if they did somethin' or not."

"Well, saves a lot of time that way. Did I pass, by the way?"

He looked down at Hastings. "You didn't kill this fella. I could see that in your eyes."

"Well, thanks, Lonesome Bob. All right if I get out of here?"

"Sure. Time Cliff gets here — he's out to the Murdoch place; dead gal in the bomb shelter, if you can believe that — I can just sit here and catch me a couple of winks."

"You look like you could use a rest."

"Law enforcement ain't no easy job, let me tell you that."

"I can see that, Lonesome Bob. I can see that."

NINE

I went outside and sat in the car and opened the package Hastings had given me that morning. My Cub Scout knife proved useful again.

I turned on the overhead light and looked inside the King Edward cigar box. It was like waiting and waiting and waiting for your birthday to arrive when you're six. And then your folks give you a temptingly wrapped package and you open it and find a dog turd.

This wasn't a turd. But it was a letdown. I had no idea what to expect but I sure didn't expect this. A receipt from the Cedar Rapids restaurant, the Embers. I studied the amount, the date, the penciled-in initials, presumably belonging to the waitress.

A strange man had given me a strange, inexplicable package to deliver. And now he was dead and so was the woman it had been intended for.

I slipped the package under my car seat,

119

got out, locked the door and walked over to the phone booth. The Judge needed an update.

"My Lord," she said. "My Lord. They've ruined their lives." She generally has snappy replies to the grimmest of griefs. She holds herself above travail, unless it's her own. She was about eight-thirty drunk. She'd be a lot more so by the time eleven rolled around. But even at eleven she'd be coherent and able to make reasonable decisions. "Ross and Gavin are good friends of mine. So are their wives. And I'm Deirdre's godmother. My Lord, this is going to sink them all." A sip of her drink, probably a martooni as Tony Randall always says in those moronic Doris Day–Rock Hudson movies my dates always insisted we see. "You don't think Ross killed her, do you?"

"I don't think so. But there's a lot I don't know yet. He could have."

"You men should all be castrated. Every one of you."

"Including all four of your ex-husbands?"

"Especially them."

Now that was more like the Judge I knew and occasionally, when I tried real hard, liked.

"For a woman. All for a woman. My

120

God, they must be insane."

"I suppose they thought it was rational. You chase around, people see you and you get a rep. You have your own concubine in an apartment that's not even in your own home town — you cut your risk a whole lot."

"Unless somebody happens to kill her and it all comes out in the investigation."

"Well," I said, "there's always that, I guess."

"I think I'm actually going to cry. I know you don't believe that, McCain. But it's true. All the lives that were ruined today. All those poor women. I even feel sorry for the men, though they don't deserve it. What a stupid idea." Another sip. "And what about the election? I hadn't even thought about that till now. Where's the party going to get another candidate?"

"Well, Republican candidates shouldn't be that hard to find. Most of them are in prisons on bunco charges."

"Hilarious wit you have there, McCain. Just hilarious."

"Well, I need to be getting on home. Been a very long day."

"All right, McCain. Good night." I had the sense that she was crying even before she hung up.

I had a burger and fries at a diner. I played four Patsy Cline songs on the counter-mounted juke box units. I tried not to think about anything except that Patsy shouldn't have had to die so young and that I'd never heard another singing voice that could quite make of loss and sadness what hers did.

Then I started thinking about Pamela. I sure hoped we were going to have sex tonight. It'd been a while for me and I was as much lonely as I was horny. Maybe I should've asked Lonesome Bob how he dealt with it all the time.

Two guys from the factory down the street came in on their nine o'clock break and ordered coffee and pie, peach for one, cherry for the other. They wore ball caps with union pins on them and denim jackets with U of Iowa Hawkeye buttons, black and gold. They made good money at their jobs. Their union had just settled a possible strike and had gotten most of what it wanted. This was a high old time in our country, the best since the end of the war. As for how it would be in the future — that was all up to Mr. Khrushchev and that feckless Russian hayseed grin of his.

"They all chipped in and paid for this whore," one of them was saying to the other as the waitress poured their coffees. "Ross Murdoch." A laugh. "I guess he won't be governor anytime soon."

"What about Ross Murdoch?" the waitress said.

"Haven't you heard the news?"

"I usually turn it on but I got treated to a Patsy Cline concert tonight." She looked right at me while she said it.

"Just be happy I didn't play Lawrence Welk," I said.

She was done with me. "So what's this about Ross Murdoch? You know, he stops in here every once in a while. Bein' political, of course. Pretendin' he's just like one of the regular folks. Mr. High and Mighty. Even when he don't try to be High and Mighty he is."

"And Hardin, too," the second man said. "And a coupla other rich boys."

"Think of that," the waitress said, after hearing the story. She put a quarter inch space between her thumb and forefinger and held them up. "He came this close to bein' governor. Can you imagine that? This close."

I waggled two rumpled dollar bills at her and dropped them next to my plate. She smiled. Sixty cents of that was a tip.

So the word was out, I thought. A scandal that would temporarily distract the public mind from the missile crisis. The end was near, at least for the four men back at Ross Murdoch's place.

I didn't know how one 110 pound woman could make all that noise. As soon as I opened the back door to my apartment and pushed inside, I found out.

One woman couldn't make all that noise. But two women can.

Ever since fourth grade, two girls have dominated my life. Sort of the way Betty and Veronica have always dominated Archie's life. The problem with that comparison being that Archie is a comic book character frozen in time. Which, come to think of it — having Betty and Veronica in their nubile prime forever — is not exactly a bad fate.

My life *isn't* frozen in time. The other day in the mirror I noticed a gray hair. Though I haven't put on any weight since college, my face isn't as sharply defined as it once was. And hanging around gas stations and talking about drag races and street rods isn't as much fun as it used to be.

And the surprises life springs on me get more and more baffling.

Sure, I'd seen my Betty and Veronica together all our lives. We were in the same classes, we went on the same class outings, we attended the same junior and senior proms. And they'd always been friendly if never exactly friends.

But I'd never seen them *together*, if you know what I mean. Never as grown women. Hell, Mary had two kids. And certainly never sitting together at the little dining table in the middle of my apartment, all three cats and a bottle of bourbon and two glasses on the table.

"She's pretty drunk," Mary said, giggling. She had that red hair ribbon in her dark hair. I could remember it as far back as senior year in high school. It brought out the sweet erotic clarity of her elegant face. She wore a buff blue blouse and jeans and white Keds tonight.

"Oh, no," the beautiful Pamela Forrest said. "She's the drunk one."

"I thought we were drinking scotch," I said.

Mary smiled. "That was gone by the time I got here. I brought this bottle. It's Johnny Walker. That's pretty good, isn't it?"

"Yeah. It's great. But —"

Easy to see that Mary was feeling nothing more than a little buzz. Pamela was the sloshed one.

Mary said, "I called to see if you were home. Pamela answered and we started talking and she asked me to come over and keep her company. My mom's watching the kids for a couple of hours. Wes's with his girlfriend."

Pamela, who could barely sit up straight, said, "He's such a jerk." Then she managed to angle her head up to me and with one eye squinting said: "We've been havin' a mighty good talk about ole McCain." Then her head made what seemed like a complete circle and she fixed me with that single blue eye again and said, "We decided that you're a very nice guy but sort of a dickhead, too."

Mary whooped a laugh. "Pamela!"

"Well, that's what we said, wasn't it?"

"That's what *you* said."

Pamela hiccoughed. "Oh, right. That's what *I* said." She tried to fling an arm in my direction but she didn't make it very far. Then she just stared at her arm as if she'd never seen it before. Then — I wasn't sure whom she was addressing here, maybe her arm — "Guy chases me ever since

126

fourth grade and then I show up at his office one day and you know what he tells me?"

Mary looked embarrassed and sorry for her. "You know, maybe you should lie down for a little bit. Not long. It doesn't have to be long. Just a little bit."

Pamela was not dissuaded. "You know what he tells me? A) That he doesn't love me any more and —" Paused. Had lost her place. "C) That he wasn't even sure he wanted to sleep with me." She leaned forward and tried to pet one of the cats. "What's her name?"

"Tasha."

"She's beautiful."

"Yes, she is."

"I'm going to get a cat," Pamela said. "I'm going to buy a sports car and get me a cat."

Then she turned vaguely in Mary's direction and said, "Any man ever turn you down before? I mean when you offered him yourself? Just *offered* yourself, no strings attached? And he turned you down?"

"Our friend McCain here used to turn me down all the time."

"See," she said, her head trying to make a complete circle again, "I told you he was a dickhead."

I swooped her up. Yep. As sure as Rhett swept up what's-her-name, I swept her up into my arms. There wasn't any grand staircase, of course, so I just carried her across the room to the double bed in the far corner and set her down on it gently.

"Hey," she said resentfully. "Hey, hey." The booze had apparently shortened her vocabulary.

I got her tennis shoes off and then her socks and then her jeans and then her blouse. "Hey," she said again.

"Sleep, Pamela."

"I came up here to have a romantic evening and look what I get."

"Sleep."

"Sit down here and hold my hand. My dad always used to do that when I was little." I'll spare you the dialect. She was slurring the words to the point of incoherence.

"Night, Pamela."

"Mary's so sweet."

"Mary's very sweet. And so are you."

"Oh, don't bullshit me, McCain. I've never been sweet a day in my life. I'm just what Stu said I was, a selfish bitch. Or self-centered. One or the other. Self-centered or selfish." Then her head flopped dramatically to the right.

By the time I was draping her jeans and blouse over the back of a chair, she was snoring.

I went back to the table and sat down and poured myself a shallow drink. I sipped it.

"I'm scared," Mary said.

"Yeah. I sensed that."

"She had this whole dream-life all planned out. She'd be with Stu and everything would be great. But the way she and Stu got together, everybody in town sees her as a homewrecker and a whore. And when she actually got to know Stu, she didn't like him at all, let alone love him." She picked up a package of Viceroys and lighted one.

"You don't smoke."

"Sometimes I do. When I get — agitated."

"And now you're agitated?"

She nodded. Looked sad. "Worried about my two kids. They need a dad."

"Wes just isn't the type to cheat."

She smiled. "You have to watch out for those moralizing types. He's always so critical of everybody else. But he's got it all rationalized. Said he thought I'd be more comfortable with his class of people. Said it wasn't my fault. Said he couldn't help it, falling in love with this woman. You know, the stuff you always say when you're trying not to hurt somebody's feelings."

"He really said you weren't comfortable with his class of people?"

"Yeah."

"This is Black River Falls, Iowa. These people with their 'class' ideas make me crazy. There's only one class of people in this town. Yokels. Hayseeds. Shitkickers. And I'm one of them and I don't have a problem with being one of them. Like being a yokel."

"I'm a yokel, too." She glanced at Pamela in bed. "Boy, if you could only see down the road. I mean, isn't it strange that the three of us would end up here together like this? I mean, if you would've predicted this, I would've said you were nuts. Pamela all passed out and not worried about her dignity or how she looks; and me with two kids and a husband who's leaving me; and you —"

"Go ahead and say it."

"Oh, Sam." She looked at me with sudden tears in her eyes. The booze. "You just sort of drift along. I saw you on the street the other day — and I almost cried. You're starting to show your age a little bit. That boyishness is starting to go. You seem — harder, I guess. I can hear that in your voice now. You're a lot more cynical and angry than you used to be. And lonelier, too. I always used to think of us — you and me — as innocents. Not like other people. That's why I always loved you. But we're different now. Both of us, I mean. You're still a lot of fun and you're so bright and everything. But I see a kind of meanness in you now, just every once in a while. But it's there." She reached over and took my hand. The touch shocked me in the literal sense. I think the hairs on my arms stood up. I know they did at the nape of my neck. "I'm sorry I said that. That's why I shouldn't drink. I always say such stupid stuff."

I didn't want to look at her the way I was looking at her but in that moment of melancholy and raw carnality it was the only way I could look at her. If you're following me.

She must have felt the same way, or sort of the same way, or at least a smidge, a bit, an iota of the same way because when I stood up, she stood up, too, and then she was in my arms and I remembered in that instant how good a kisser she was. She had been talking about how things could turn out so strange sometimes and right now I couldn't think of anything stranger than the former love of my life sleeping in my bed in her bra and panties while I was making out with the second love of my life in the middle of the floor.

But we weren't in the middle of the floor for long. Soon enough we were on the couch and firing our clothes every which direction. No chance Pamela was going to wake up and interrupt us.

The first time was quick and explosive. We found out just how lonely we really were. We had to grab it before it got away. Like those first times back in high school when, in the middle of it, all you thought was *McCain, you dipshit; you're actually having sex. Real live sex with a real live girl. No more brief visits to the john with a sheet torn from Mr. Hefner's magazine jammed in your back pocket. Yes, McCain. Real live sex.* The second time was gentler and slower. And then we lay naked under a blanket on the couch and watched part of an old movie — something with Jean Arthur — and she said, "I should feel terrible about this."

"Why?"

"I'm married, Sam. I'm the faithful type."

"He has another woman."

"Yes, but still —"

"Catholic school. It never lets you go. There's no reason to feel guilty."

"I s'pose you're right." Then, "You think I could come back sometime?"

"I'm sorry. We're closed for the summer."

"You're joking but you're not joking. Do you really want me to come back?"

"Sure." But I knew I sounded *un*sure.

"Don't worry, Sam. I don't have any — you know, expectations. I'm lonely and you're lonely and that's all it has to mean."

"I care about you."

"I know you do. And maybe some day —"

But she didn't get a chance to finish the sentence because somebody was coming up the back stairs. And then pounding on the door frame. If he'd have pounded on the glass, he would have smashed it.

"Who's that?" Mary said, as alarmed as I was.

I quickly rolled off the couch and started throwing her clothes at her. I jerked my clothes on, doing a one-legged job so I could get my trousers on faster.

The thunderous knocking.

So thunderous that the cats were jumping off the table and heading for cover.

Mary rushing to the bathroom.

Me grabbing my .38 and jamming it into my back pocket.

Him getting in one more rock-crushing knock before I reached the door.

He was bigger than I remembered. And he was angry. Jealous-angry. No man, however meek, is more dangerous than when he's jealous of his woman and suspecting she's with another man. He'd never been meek. And even now in his gray topcoat and blue suit and white shirt and blue-striped tie, he looked as if he could get twenty yards from scrimmage with the Bears.

"Where's Pamela?"

I raised my hand and pointed. Moses couldn't have done it more dramatically when he pointed out the promised land.

"You sonofabitch!" he said.

At this point, Pamela had pushed off the covers and was lying in her skimpies in a position that would drive subscribers to Mr. Hefner's magazine insane.

He took a swing at me, which was a mistake because I pulled my .38 and stuck it in his face. "Good thing you didn't connect, Stu, because I could mess you up pretty bad without firing a shot. And I sure as hell wouldn't mind doing it. Now get hold of yourself and shut up while I tell you what's going on here."

Mary opened the bathroom door and peeked out. "Sam and Pamela didn't do anything, Stu, if that's what you were thinking."

"What the hell're you doing here, Mary? You're a married woman."

She came out of the bathroom. She had combed her hair, put on fresh lipstick. She looked pretty damned wonderful. "He left me for somebody else."

"Wes? Wes Lindstrom?" he said. "My God, he was one of the most upstanding people in the whole town. What's gone wrong with this place? Has everybody lost his sense of decency? My wife lying there in her underwear. And you Mary up here with — with McCain." He made "McCain" sound very dirty. Stu was another local Brahmin. I was not fit for local society.

"Stu, before you get all set up in the pulpit up there," I said, "let me remind you that you left your wife and kids and ran off with Pamela. That means you don't get to judge people the way you're judging Mary and me. Or anybody else, for that matter."

"You didn't sleep with Pamela?"

"I didn't sleep with her."

"It still pisses me off that she came running back to you."

"She's confused."

He touched his hand to his head. I figured he either had a headache or was fighting back tears. "I never should've left my wife and kids like that. My kids haven't forgiven me yet, I'm not sure they ever will. Of course their mother poisons their minds against me every day."

"How do you know that?"

"I talk to them on the phone all the time. They tell me some of the things their mother tells them. Man, I'm Hitler and Stalin rolled into one."

He gaped at the bed again. "You really didn't sleep with her?"

"I really didn't sleep with her."

"But I'll bet you wanted to."

"Oh, Lord, Stu," Mary said. "You practically break in here and start accusing Sam of all sorts of things when he tells you over and over that he and Pamela didn't do anything. He's telling you the truth. I was here the whole time."

He walked over to her and put his hand on her shoulder. "You're one of the nicest people in this town, Mary. Why McCain here didn't marry you is beyond me."

She laughed. "It's beyond me, too."

He saw the bottle on the table. "Mind if I have a snort?"

"Be my guest," Mary said.

He had two snorts. Once, he sobbed. A single sob. It just sort of escaped. And then you could see him force himself to stop. He made a fist, he made a face, he said, "Shit, this is great, isn't it?"

"Just calm down, Stu."

"Calm down? I'm back in this town where everybody hates me. My wife wants to leave me. And I'm making an ass out of myself in front of Mary and you."

"Stu," I said, "I've made an ass of myself in front of so many people, they'd fill a stadium."

His face showed surprise. "Really?"

"Hell, yes, if I don't make an ass of myself at least twice a day, I can't sleep at night. I just lie there and think of all the opportunities I missed."

He gave me his courtroom smile. Before he'd wrecked his legal career by fleeing town with a woman named the beautiful Pamela Forrest, he'd been one of the highest paid attorneys in the state. There was talk of the governor's mansion or at least a state supreme court appointment. "You're being a lot nicer to me than you should be. One more?"

"Be my guest."

He poured. He drank. He sighed. "And

all this insane stuff with Ross Murdoch and his three buddies. Keeping a woman. Incredible. I knew it'd all catch up to them some day." He took one more drink. "He said he'd nail them."

"Who?"

"Little guy. They had a magic act. I met her when she first came out here, but I didn't know why she was here. But her brother did. He found out what she was up to. I heard them arguing as I was leaving the courthouse one day. She'd been in the driver's license bureau, I guess. Anyway, I was waiting for an elevator and just stood in the hall while they kept going. That's how I found out what she was really doing about it."

"He was mad because she was a concubine?"

"Hell, no. He was mad because she was cutting him out of the money. She'd done things like this in the past but he always got some of the proceeds. He kept shouting that he didn't have a magic act or a woman to sell."

"I'll be damned," I said.

"At this rate, McCain," he said, pointing a final time to the bottle for permission, "we'll all be damned."

TEN

I wasn't ready for sleep. They were half an hour gone and I sat in the easy chair with the warm remains of a beer and my little ten cent Woolworth notebook that fits just about any pocket you care to name.

I was making one of my famous lists, the way this cop had taught us in night school. He said there were two kinds of forms you should fill out for every incident. The official one, for which the state provided the form. And your own, which you provided for yourself. He urged us to make up our own form. He said, for instance, to use emotional words when you were conducting an investigation. I kept the example he gave us tucked into every one of my notebooks.

AL DUFFY
Arrogant
Evasive
Wife afraid of him

Say this was a fire investigation and you're the detective assigned to liaison with the fire department folks. The first thing they'll want to eliminate is arson, which is generally motivated by money or revenge. When you look at Al Duffy's attributes (as you perceive them), you'll look doubly close at the possibility of arson just because of his attitude. The way he bullies his wife with angry glances and interruptions may be significant here. Maybe she's on the verge of confessing to what they've done.

I made my own list.

ROSS MURDOCH
Distracted
Depressed
Afraid

MIKE HARDIN
Angry
Frantic

Then I stopped myself. These little profiles were going to be essentially the same for all of them. Who wouldn't be distracted, depressed, afraid? Who wouldn't be angry and frantic?

I should be writing down motives instead of moods.

But why would any of them kill their hired woman and her brother? Their deaths guaranteed that the whole setup would become public and destroy them.

It was more likely that somebody who hated one or all of them had found out about their concubine and decided to inflict the worst kind of revenge — public humiliation and the destruction of their reputations. Plus there was a good chance that one or two of them might even be tried for murder.

Men like these would have made innumerable enemies. Some deserved, some not. Successful people are targets.

But if it was revenge, then it was done by somebody who'd really thought everything through. He would have had to murder the woman, hide her body in a container and then get inside the house.

Daunting as this seemed, it certainly wasn't impossible with all those workmen going in and out. The men would be working for several different companies, so what was one more man from one more company? He'd have to go in at the very end of the day, of course. If Murdoch was telling me the truth and really hadn't gone down to the shelter between approximately five p.m. and the next morning (a fact I'd noted in my notebook), then all the killer had to do was sit back and wait. Think of Murdoch's face when he saw the dead woman. Think of Murdoch's panic. His shame.

I went to bed around three o'clock. I read fifty pages of the new Charles Williams Gold Medal novel which was, as always, well-crafted and fetchingly written. There was a darkness in Williams's books that you couldn't find even in Jim Thompson. Thompson's darkness was the darkness of the insane. Williams's darkness was the darkness of the sane. A subtler and ultimately more terrifying doom.

I lay in the luxury of Pamela's various scents — sleep, body heat, perfume. I got a useless erection and then fell asleep, my second-to-last thought being that in the morning I needed to get a list of all the companies that had worked on the bomb shelter. My very last thought was to wonder if Mike Hardin's financial loss in any way played into the murders. But I was too tired to puzzle it through.

I had breakfast in the café down the street from my office. I had the waitress pour the coffee directly into my eyes. You wake up faster that way.

No need to wonder what the various conversations were about. There is nothing quite so pleasing as watching the mighty fall. And if they fall because of a sex scandal it's really a lot of fun. Like hearing that John Wayne was really a transvestite. You know — that shadow between the public image and the private person. A few years ago *Confidential* magazine had made a lot of money with just such tales.

From what I could hear, the murder wasn't nearly as interesting to the downtown folks as the idea that they'd hired the woman to share sex. The double homicides would play in later. But for now the whole idea of having your own kept woman — this was the stuff of legend. It was good for at least three generations and maybe more. Who cared about dead people when you had a beautiful lady putting out for the four men who kept her in relative luxury?

I was at the counter, paying my bill, when Deirdre came in. The morning was chilly enough to rouge her cheeks with wholesome red spots and to draw silver dragon-breath from her perfect little nostrils. "I went to your office. Decided I'd just start walking up and down the street. I really need to talk to you." She wore movie star sunglasses, very dark and provocative.

A lot of the patrons knew who she was. It became a bad cowboy movie suddenly. The gunfighter everybody's afraid of walks in and conversation goes silent. Everybody watching. Staring.

She kept her eyes averted. If she looked at them, it would just reconfirm the hell her life had become. There was a fifteen-year-old boy whose father had shotgunned and raped a waitress. The mother was too ashamed — and angry — to attend the trial. I was hired as the public defender. The father was the kind of bully who probably should have been drowned when he was a couple months old. Definitely mentally deformed. But the boy was there. Every day. Sat right up in the first pew, too. Just wanted his old man — abominable as he was — to know that there was still blood between them and that he was there to offer the man his support. All the smirks and name-calling and even threats the kid had to endure — but by God he was there every day the court was in session. When the Amish drive someone from their community, they do so by "shunning" them. The kid had been shunned but he stood up to it.

I wondered how Deirdre was going to

fare. She was definitely going to be shunned. And for a long, long time.

"Let's go back to my office," I said.

As we walked she said, "I look like hell."

"You're right about that. You're one of the ugliest women I've ever known."

She laughed. "My father's life is crumbling down around him and I'm worried about my looks. God, am I vain."

"You have reason to be vain."

"Keep talking like that."

"How're your folks holding up?"

"Dad's angry. Last night he was depressed. Now he's angry. I'll take angry any day. My mom's always depressed. She's been seeing a shrink in Iowa City for years. That I'm used to. But Dad's almost never depressed. He takes action. I think men do that — busy themselves, even if what they're doing doesn't amount to much."

We were at my office. Went inside. It was cold. I turned on the heat. I sat in my Philip Marlowe chair and she sat across from me.

"So what's going on?"

She bowed her head for a time. Said nothing. I thought maybe she was praying silently. "Dad has an alibi for the night before last. The night the coroner says the

Hastings woman was murdered. He also has an alibi for last night, when her brother was murdered."

"Then he's in the clear. With criminal charges, I mean. His political career —"

"He doesn't even mention that any more. He's calling a press conference for this afternoon. He'll pull out of the race."

"But you sound like there's a problem."

"It's Mom. She stayed in bed this morning and started doubling up on her tranquilizer. This might go on for weeks. She may even end up back in the nuthouse again."

"She was in a mental hospital?"

"She takes 'trips.' She always says she's going to California to visit one of her sisters that lives there. But she and this sister haven't spoken in years. She's really going to this hospital in Chicago. The last time, she was so far down she rode the lightning, as they call it."

"Shock treatments?"

"A dozen of them. God, I felt so sorry for her."

"Isn't that a pretty radical step, electroshock?"

"Not as radical as you'd think. My minor was psych. They do shock treatments on all kinds of people now. And this time —"

She paused. "Well, it was a special circumstance that time. She took a couple of shots at Dad. Well, sort of."

"Are you serious?"

"Unfortunately, yes. Another one of his dalliances. Some woman he'd spent some time with in Chicago a few years back sent him a birthday card. He must be sleeping with mental defectives. Who'd send a birthday card to a married man? Anyway, Mom just flipped out. Grabbed the gun he keeps in his desk drawer, went into the den and fired twice at him. I don't think she meant to actually hurt him. He always gets dramatic about it and says 'that time she tried to kill me.' But my grandfather taught all three of his girls how to shoot and mom's pretty good at it. If she'd wanted to kill Dad, she could have."

"So you're worried —"

"She could be a suspect. She's — fragile. You wouldn't know it. She's usually very good at keeping up a front. But — I just had to get your opinion."

"We're all just sitting here waiting to see how this plays out. I'm going on with my investigation. Right now I really don't have any opinion. I need more facts."

"I know. I was just hoping you had some idea." She shook her head. "Check that.

It's a lie. I needed to get out of that house. God, you can't believe what it's like in there. And I just keep picturing the Hastings woman down in the bomb shelter — I just needed to get out of there. So I came looking for you." She stood up. "I saw you keep looking at the notes on your desk. Which means that you're very busy and that I'm in the way. But I feel better just talking to you."

"I'm glad of that," I said. "I just wish I could come up with something helpful."

"I'm half-tempted to see if I could get Mom back in the hospital again. Away from all this."

"Would she go?"

"She might." I walked her to the door. She kissed me on the mouth. Her lipstick tasted good and her mouth was wonderful. She never had taken her shades off. "Thanks, Sam."

"Good luck to both of us."

ELEVEN

I spent nearly eighty minutes on the phone. I contacted the companies Ross Murdoch had given me. And from the companies I got the names of the men who'd worked on building the bomb shelter. I also got the addresses of where they were working today.

I spent two hours driving around town talking to them, much to the displeasure of their bosses. I kept my visits as short as possible. Most of the men said the same thing. That people came and went all day long during the construction process and they really didn't pay much attention. Same thing about the day of the murder. Hadn't paid much attention.

One man said he'd noticed a red-haired sheet metal guy with a blue eagle tattoo on the top of his right hand. That was the guy from Palmer Sheet Metal I'd interview later. Another guy told me he'd seen a Negro man late in the day carry a big box to the back door. I wrote down what he told me and then called the Murdoch house. Deirdre was there. She said the man was from a furniture store and that she had signed for the chair he carried herself. A third possibility evaporated even faster. An electrician told me that he'd seen a green truck pull up just before quitting time. The Murdochs had requested that all the workers be out of there promptly at six every evening. I called Deirdre back. She said that the long cardboard container from that particular truck was a floor lamp. They'd hired a decorator and all the items she'd selected for the revamp were just being delivered in the past few days. A lot of other people in and out, too.

"It must be frustrating," she said.

"It is. But it's usually the only way to learn things." Then: "How's your mom?"

"Sleeping. I've checked on her twice. I just hope she stays asleep."

"How's your dad?"

"Nervous. He's giving a press conference on the steps of the court house in another hour. He's in the den going over and over his prepared statement. He's going to get everything out in the open. I know he made this mess all by himself — and that he's a grown-up and so on and so forth —

but I still feel sorry for him. He's a very proud man. And some of the people in this town'll eat him alive."

"Unfortunately, I think you're right. I'm sorry for your family."

"Dad says that he deserves it. He was really morose a while ago. He said it would be better for everybody if he just dropped dead. His side of the family has a history of heart trouble. That's one of the reasons he stays in such good shape."

"Tell him I'll be checking in with him tonight by phone."

"I was hoping to see you."

"I have a feeling I'm going to be working straight through the night."

"So what will you do now?"

"Start talking to the other three men, one by one."

"I don't envy you that. They're not easy to deal with. I've been around them all my life. They can really give you a hard time."

"Gosh, I find that hard to believe."

"Poor Sam," she said. "Poor, poor Sam."

I tried Mike Hardin, office and home. Not in. I tried Gavin Wheeler, office and home. Not in. I tried Peter Carlson. The country club golf course.

In big cities, country clubs are usually

formidable places. A lot of them are designed to intimidate. I've seen some as big and excessive as Rhineland castles. The Cedar View Country Club isn't quite there yet. It's a large, one-story, flat-roofed building made out of native stone. The members built it with an eye to expansion so there's a lot more parking space than they need currently. The golf course, I'm told, is pretty decent for a town this size. The hot summer had scorched most of the grass brown. The leaves were just starting to turn autumnal. You could see geese and pheasants and hawks against the hard blue sky.

I found a caddy and said, "Five bucks if you'll do me a favor."

He was in his forties, stooped slightly from his occupation, and was not as subservient as some of the members probably expected. I'm one of those people who can kiss ass for fifty-eight minutes if I really have to. But make it fifty-nine and I get surly. All the groveling backs up in my throat and starts to burn.

I think the fortyish caddie with the frayed yellow cotton cap and the checkered brown-and-yellow pants had just reached his own fifty-nine minutes. He said, with great weariness, "I sure hope I don't have to walk far. I got a scratchy throat — my oldest daughter came home from school yesterday throwin' up and sayin' it hurt to swallow. I think I'm comin' down with it myself."

"You know where Peter Carlson is?"

His mouth twisted into a frown when I mentioned the name. Carlson treated lessers without mercy. And every person on the planet was his lesser. Then he grinned with two neat rows of dentures. "Between us, tell you where I'd like him to be."

"Guess a lot of people feel that way."

"Most everybody out here does. Even the big shots."

"You go get him for me? I don't have a membership here and I don't know the course well enough to find him."

"Twenty bucks?"

"Whatever happened to charity toward your fellow man?"

"I don't make enough money to be charitable." The smile again. I paid him.

He came back in twelve minutes by my watch.

"He says call him at the office, he's playing golf."

"Figured that might happen."

"Tell you what. Since I wasn't able to bring him back, give me a tenner and call it even." He handed me back the twenty I'd given him and took the ten I was holding out.

"Fair enough. Thanks."

On the drive back to my office, I started thinking those tricky, Agatha Christie thoughts that always come up when more sensible ones don't.

There's this furniture truck, see. And the driver and his assistant stop for coffee, see. And there's this guy following them in his car, see. And he's got this body in this box, see. Well, what he does, while they're having coffee — they parked near the back, see, where nobody can see him do this — so he takes his box and slides it up in the back of the truck and he hops up there himself. Then he rides out to the Murdoch place and before the driver comes to a complete stop, he jumps down. Then he takes his box and hurry-fast takes it down to the bomb shelter. All the while looking like just one more workman. Then he speeds off into the nearby woods and nobody ever sees him again.

A ten-year-old can pick the flaws out in that plan. So much depends on sheer good luck, exquisite timing and coincidence that it could only work in an old-fashioned mystery novel.

Gavin Wheeler was nice enough to open my office door for me. "You should get a better lock."

"Thanks for the advice. You should get a better lawyer. Maybe he could get breaking and entering dropped to criminal mischief."

Wheeler smirked. "I would've taken something, McCain, but there isn't nothing worth taking in this shithole."

I went in and sat behind the desk — it was my office, after all — checked with the phone service who said that nobody had called. While I was doing this, Wheeler, looking like a Texas oil man in a good brown suit and a white shirt with a strong tie and a white Stetson, worked on emptying a silver flask of its contents. I had reason to suspect there wasn't Kool-Aid in there. He kept making this irritating sound "Ah!" after every hit. Apparently the flask, of modest size, was of a magical nature. It never seemed to reach empty.

He said, "I didn't kill her. Or him. And this whole idea I was opposed to from the start. The broad, I mean."

"I see. They forced you into it."

"In a way they did. I'm not like the other three, McCain. I believe in God and I go to church. And I don't go to church just because it looks good. It's because I feel it. In here." He tapped his chest as if he had indigestion. "And in a way, they did force me into it."

"I see."

"You can sit there and smirk at me all you want. But it's the truth. Those three, they grew up with money. Hell, Murdoch, he even went to Dartmouth. Me, I never finished high school."

"I'm not sure what this has to do with the two murders, Mr. Wheeler."

"Gavin, please."

It's kind of strange. People who ordinarily wouldn't even speak to you want you to call them by their first names when they get into trouble.

"You want to know what my background has to do with those two murders? I'll tell you. When you come from where I come from — those shanties where the Southerners lit during the Depression, them tin shacks and you know what I'm talking about — you never feel quite right about yourself. And don't tell me you don't know what I'm talkin' about, McCain, because you're from the Hills and you know how that affects you. Deep down, you never feel as good as other people. Deep down, you're ashamed of yourself and you can't ever kick that feeling. No matter how much money you have; no matter how many people tell you how great you are; no matter how many civic awards they give you — inside here you know you could lose it all at any minute. The money, the prestige, the rich friends — all gone like that." He snapped his fingers. "I walk around with that feeling in the pit of my stomach every day of my life. That's where I envy you so much."

"You envy me?"

"Hell, yes, I do. Look at you. You don't have jack shit. Your law practice is a joke and all you do most of the time is play gumshoe for some old wino judge who has to tell you ten times a day that she knows Leonard Bernstein. You're about the most unsuccessful professional man in this whole state and you should be damned happy about it."

"God, I never realized how lucky I was. Every time I have to prowl through garbage cans to get my dinner, I should realize that I've got it made. Something like that?"

"Now you're being sarcastic again. And you know what? That's about the only thing you're good at. That sarcasm of yours."

I sat up with my elbows on the desk, leaning forward the way those TV actors do when they're selling you a product of some kind. "First of all, Gavin, you forgot about the Hills as soon as you left. All those years you were on the city council you didn't do squat for the Hills. Hell, you even blocked all the sewage bills so your country club friends could get the council to build that sports park we didn't need. And second of all, you're here to rat out somebody else to throw suspicion off yourself. You're going to give me a name and some little morsel of a lead and I'm supposed to get excited."

He took his flask out again and set it on the desk. "Take a drink of that, McCain. And while you're doin' that, I'll tell you who killed those two people."

"Sure you will."

"Two weeks ago somebody beat up Karen."

"And you know that for a fact?"

"Hell, yes I know it for a fact. It was my night to be with her. Two of us a week. That was the setup. More than that she would've felt like a whore. This way she could pretend she just had two dates a week."

"She say that?"

"Many times. Anyway, I saw the bruises

158

all over her body. First hand."

"Who did it?"

"Peter Carlson."

"C'mon. Carlson?"

"Why's that so hard to believe?"

"He's sort of a priss. Hard to imagine him working up that kind of passion for anything except putting people down."

"Well, whatever he is, that didn't stop him from falling in love with her."

"Are you serious?"

"He offered to buy out our shares. He even tried to get her to move back to Chicago, where he'd set her up by himself."

"When did all this happen?"

"Over the last couple months. He had a hard time controlling himself when one of us went up there. Sometimes he'd drive around her block. I know it's hard to believe but that's how bad he got. He even picked a fight with Hardin one night when they were both drinking. Hardin made some crack about her starting to show her age a little bit. And speaking of cracks, I didn't forget about the Hills. I give three Christmas baskets to the nuns every year. For the poor."

"Be still my heart."

"It'd be real easy not to like you, McCain."

"Ditto. Why don't you just take this to Cliffie?"

"That dumb ass? Are you kidding? He's already got Murdoch good for it. You know Cliffie. Case closed. He won't even consider anybody else now."

I leaned back in my chair. Watched him tilt his flask up again. Watched him set it back down on the desk. Watched him watching me.

"You going to help me clear Ross? Ross said you were working for him."

"What if I find out you killed her?"

His jowls got red before the rest of his face did. An interesting visual display. "Why would I kill her?"

"Well, Cliffie thinks Ross killed her. You say Carlson killed her. And I'm sure somebody'll tell me they think Mike Hardin killed her. Your name's bound to come up sometime."

"Well, I didn't and I can prove it. I was in a poker game till almost two o'clock. And I was drunk enough that I had one of the other guys give me a ride home."

"He got a name, this guy?"

"You're a jerk, you know that, McCain."

"You want me to help Ross, I'm helping Ross. I'm trying to find the killer."

"I'm not the killer."

"I need the name of the guy who drove you home."

He sat back. He seemed to shrink. He aged by a few years. He looked embarrassed. "I was making that up about the poker game."

"You got any other alibis? Shacked up with Jackie Kennedy or something like that?"

He stood up. "I was home. Watching TV and pretty drunk. The wife was upstairs asleep."

"So you don't have an alibi."

"I was home."

"You could always leave home."

"I was drunk."

"So you say."

"This is all because of that sewer thing, isn't it?"

"A good part of it, anyway."

"I don't vote for sewer improvement so you're going to hang a murder rap on me?"

"You even voted against extending services to the people down by the river. Of any kind. That's pretty shitty." I leaned forward on my elbows again. "I'm not going to hang anything on you that doesn't fit. But it wouldn't break my heart if it turned out you killed those two people."

He walked to the door. Started to say

something. Got all red-faced again. And then left.

I spent the next hour working on my notebook list. I hadn't been kidding when I said that I expected to hear from Peter Carlson and Mike Hardin. They'd be implicating one of their friends just as Wheeler had. The panic had crazed them. It didn't matter who was ultimately blamed as far as their reputations went. They were already destroyed merely by association with the dead woman and her brother.

The phone rang.

"What time you coming home?" the beautiful Pamela Forrest said.

"I don't know. Another couple hours. Why?"

"We, uh, wondered if we could make you a business offer."

" 'We' being?"

"We being Stu and me."

"What kind of business offer?"

"Well, we're still at your apartment. And we started talking. And — well, we wondered if we paid you motel rates, could we stay here?"

"You mean sleep there and everything?"

"Yes. You could take the couch. And it'd only be a few nights."

"Why don't you just get a motel room?"

"Because somebody'd spot us for sure. And we're not ready to face up to everything yet. It's going to be terrible. It's going to be like the Salem Witch Trials. And guess who's the witch?"

"Oh, man, I don't know."

"You don't have to worry about the sex. I mean we kinda caught up during the day today."

"That's nice to know. I'm glad I'm not in love with you any more. I mean, if I was, that's not the sort of thing I'd want to hear."

"Well, you told me you weren't in love with me so I'm taking you at your word."

"Well, maybe I'm still in love with you a little bit. A smidge. An iota."

"Well, I took that into account. That's why I didn't go into any details. You know, tell you how many times we did it or anything."

"That was very nice of you."

I could hear her getting a cigarette going. "Stu's not here right now. He took the back road into Iowa City. He's getting groceries. He's going to fix dinner for all three of us. He makes the best steaks I've ever had."

"You know, I used to hate Stu. And now

he'll be sleeping in my bed. And with you."

"Well, he used to hate you, too. In fact, I think he still does in a small sort of way."

"Well, since we're being honest here, I think I still hate him in a small sort of way."

"Well, there you have it."

"Have what?"

"You're even up. He still hates you in a small sort of way and you still hate him in a small sort of way."

"I want a new bed."

"What?"

"Before you leave, I want $75 for a new bed. I know where I can get a good one for that." I'd been planning on replacing the lumpy bed I had. And here was a chance to get a new one for free.

"I'll have to ask Stu."

As we hung up, I tried very hard not to picture Pamela and Stu in my bed. You really never can predict life's twists and turns. And that's what makes life so exhilarating and terrifying at the same time. And if you don't believe me, just ask the Three Stooges. Curly almost never knows when Mo's going to hit him.

For two hours I canvassed the apartment complex where Karen Hastings had lived.

The three buildings were red brick with a central section between that held a swimming pool and flagstone-floored social area. It was getting cold for outdoor activities. Most of the residents were in their twenties, single, and worked in either Cedar Rapids or Iowa City. Several of the apartments were rented by small groups of young women who couldn't afford the address otherwise. It was all piss elegant. *Striving* is the correct word here. It strove to be fancy and big city and sexy but it didn't quite make it because the design was strictly Apartment House 101 and the workmanship was terrible. Joints didn't fit right. Door handles were loose. The indoor carpeting was already worn thin. And pieces of the hall trim had already fallen off and not been replaced.

Two of the young women were stewardesses who flew out of Cedar Rapids. Joan Cawlings was the one I talked to. Her roommate was in the shower the whole time I was there.

Joan was a slight blonde with enormous blue eyes. She wore a U of Illinois T-shirt. She had very merry, happy little breasts that looked as though they'd be a lot of fun to play with. She wore a pair of jeans that fit her wonderfully as only jeans can. Her small feet — pert as baby rabbits — were bare.

"I think I talked to her once in the seven months I've been living here. Everybody said that she was almost hostile. A lot of people thought she was a prostitute. Different men were always coming here."

I described them.

She nodded. "Yes. Those men and one other."

"Could you describe him?"

"He looked like a boxer. Not mean or a crook or anything like that. But his nose was sort of flattened and just the way he carried himself — he was probably in his forties but one of the guys I was seeing said 'That's somebody to walk wide of.' I remember his exact words because they sounded like something from a cowboy movie. Walking wide of somebody, I mean."

"How often did you see him?"

"Well, when I first moved in, I didn't see him that much. With my schedule, it's hard to say. Maybe he came a lot when I was working. But the last couple months, I've seen him a lot more often."

"Anything different you notice about him?"

"His Corvette."

I wrote that down in my notebook. "What about it?"

"He had one of those little things you put on your license plate. It says 'MD.' You know, medical doctor. That's why he always struck me as interesting. He sort of looked like a boxer but he was always dressed in very good suits. And he drove this black Corvette. And you could tell he took very good care of it."

"How's that?"

"You never saw a speck of dust on it. And it always looked like he'd just gotten done shining it." Then: "God, when I heard her name on the radio this morning — and heard how those four men had set her up here — I'm from Cleveland so I guess I always thought of this area as kind of hicky if you know what I mean. And no offense if you grew up here or anything. But I've never heard of anything like this even in Cleveland. You know, you wouldn't be surprised if it happened in Paris or Hollywood or some place like that. But here —"

"This is great."

"It is?"

"Finding a doctor who drives a black Corvette shouldn't be too tough."

"I actually thought he was the coolest

guy of all of them. The ones who called on her, I mean. He's kinda sexy, actually."

I thanked her and walked to the door.

"Say," she said, "anything new with the missiles?"

"Nothing that I've heard of."

"The company is warning us what to do if a missile hits a city we're supposed to land in. It's really scary."

That detail made the whole crisis even more real. You never think of things like that. You're in a plane thirty thousand feet up and the city below you becomes a mushroom cloud. Then what?

"Thanks again," I said.

TWELVE

I had a beer at a tavern with animal heads on the wall. The way I feel about hunting is I'd rather see the hunters' heads on the wall. But I don't suppose I'll ever get to be president of the United States saying things like that now, will I? Or didn't I tell you that I have this diabolical plan to take over the United States?

I called a friend of mine on the Cedar Rapids police force and asked him to run a check on the black Corvette driven by a doctor.

Then I dawdled over a second beer, not wanting to go back to my apartment, which was turning into a crime scene, the crime being French farce. The woman I'd loved most of my life sleeping with the man I'd hated most of my life under my roof? God either has a great sense of humor or none at all. When I figure out which it is, I'll get back to you.

On the third and final beer — I am not a

great drinker — I decided, and I think truthfully, that I didn't love Pamela any more. I know you're not supposed to trust beery revelations but there was something dead inside me now where she was concerned — I started thinking of all the F. Scott Fitzgerald short stories I'd read in college where the protagonist ends with something dead inside where his woman is concerned — but when I thought of her now I just felt a sadness. Even though she'd never loved me, she'd been the center of my life all those years. But she wasn't now and never would be again and I felt alone in a way I'd never felt before.

Screw it, I thought. They could have my apartment. I'd stay at a motel. I'd only go over there in the morning to shower and change clothes. Hell, I'd get a new bed out of it for my trouble and a good motel room would be eight, nine bucks was all. I'd come out ahead.

Stu answered when I called and I told him what I had in mind.

"But I'm making steaks."

"More for you."

"Jeez, McCain, this doesn't seem right. Kicking you out of your own apartment."

"You're not kicking me out. I am. And

by the way, the bed you're going to buy me?"

"Uh-huh."

"I want a one hundred dollar bed."

"That's no problem."

"Great. Then I'll see you in the morning. Oh — did I get any calls?"

"Hang on a sec." Though he cupped the phone, I heard him say, "Did he get any calls?"

"Kenny Thibodeau. That dirty book writer." She'd never much approved of Kenny.

"That dirty book writer. You know, Kenny."

"Fine. I'll talk to you in the morning."

There wasn't any answer at Kenny's place so I walked down the street to an Italian restaurant, the only ethnic restaurant in town except the one where they serve buffalo burgers. I'm not sure which ethnicity that is. Eskimo?

I ate a plate full of damned good spaghetti and started pouring down coffee. I don't like the feeling of being drunk. The coffee and a bunch of Luckies helped me sober up. My dad has the same problem. When you're as small as we are, you don't hold your booze well. It's a shameful thing for a Celt to admit.

One table away, a working class family of five were discussing the missile crisis. The littlest girl was so scared she started to cry. She crawled up in her daddy's lap and he kissed her on top of her blonde curly head and then he sort of rocked her as he probably had when she was a baby. It broke my heart. And made me angry. Some guy somewhere in this place called Russia gets pissed off because some guy somewhere in this place called America was stupid enough to listen to the CIA and invade Cuba. Or try to. It sure as hell wasn't much of an invasion. And so this guy in Russia, in a snit because of it, decides to play poker with nuclear warheads as chips. And maybe destroy or at least alter life on this planet for the next 50,000 years. Awfully damned hard to explain that to a little girl in Black River Falls, Iowa who's too young to understand where Russia is or why the CIA was run by zealots who didn't much care about lives, American or otherwise, or why her mom suddenly started crying last night when they all got down on their knees and said the rosary for world peace.

I got up and went for a walk. The cold night air felt good. The Johnny Cash song wailing out of the tavern sounded mighty lonely.

After my walk, I went to a corner grocery store and bought two Pepsis, a package of smokes and a paperback by a new guy named Dan J. Marlowe, who was one mighty fine writer. Fifteen minutes later, I was in my motel room in my underwear and under the blankets, reading my book.

After fifty excellent pages, I tried Kenny again. This time he answered.

"Heard something I thought I'd pass on."

"Great. What is it?"

"Mrs. Murdoch tried to pay off Karen Hastings. To get her out of town. Mrs. Murdoch has plenty of money of her own. Her husband didn't know anything about it. She started at ten thousand but the Hastings woman said no. So eventually she went to twenty thousand. I think she copped to the whole thing, man. The four guys and Karen Hastings, I mean."

"Hold on a sec."

I dug out my notebook and wrote it down.

"That's useful. Thanks. I don't suppose you'll tell me who you heard it from?"

"Can't. I took the Boy Scout oath."

"You could be making all this stuff up. How would I know?"

"Would the author of *The Torrid Twins* ever lie to you?"

"I thought that was *The Tempting Twins.*"

"They changed the title for the second edition."

"Ah."

"See what you can do with it, anyway. She might have iced the Hastings dame."

"Boy, you're really picking up on the tough-guy talk."

"Yeah, I'm digging the hell out of this detective gig, man."

I tried to go back to reading, I wanted to go back to reading, I told myself that I *should* go back to reading and put everything else out of my mind for the evening —

But since I already had my notebook at hand —

I started going through motives that might lead an unstable mind to commit two murders.

Mike Hardin

Gavin Wheeler

Peter Carlson
Wanted her for himself

Ross Murdoch
Brother shaking him down for money

Mrs. Murdoch
Wanted her out of town

I fell asleep just before the ten o'clock news, not waking up until just before six. I dressed in yesterday's clothes and drove over to my place.

I let myself in, being as quiet as possible. I opened the door to the meows of the three cats who stared up at me with long, guilt-inducing gazes. How dare I spend the night somewhere else? But I could see their bowls from here. They'd been fed well and their water had been refreshed and filled to the brim in the bowl.

A voice said, "Don't worry about us. We've been up all night."

I walked into the area that I used as the living room. Stu sat on the couch, smoking a cigarette. He wore pajamas and his hair was mussed and he needed a shave. A pillow was propped up against the arm of the couch. On the opposite end was a blanket.

"I slept on the couch."

"Why?"

"I'll tell you why. Because I'm leaving him."

The beautiful Pamela Forrest was sitting up in the middle of my bed. She too wore pajamas and her hair was mussed. She didn't need a shave.

"Why're you leaving him?"

"Why? We patched things up last night and I told him I loved him and was glad he'd come back to get me. And then I told him about this art class I was taking and it started all over again."

"What started all over again?"

She gave him a disgusted look and said, "You tell him, Stu. And then just listen to yourself."

Stu seemed embarrassed. "Well."

"Well, he got jealous. As usual. That's why I left him. When I said our marriage wasn't what I'd imagined it would be? Well, that's the real reason. All those other reasons I gave you all boil down to this, McCain. He's so jealous he wants to keep me locked up all the time."

"What's wrong with art classes, Stu?"

"You don't know her, McCain. The way she flirts. She takes an art class — especially one at night — I'll lose her for sure. I mean, back here, I didn't have any competition. No offense, McCain. I mean, nothing personal. But I was the only guy she was interested in. But in Chicago —"

"That's why I'm leaving him, McCain. 'The way she flirts.' God, I never flirt."

"The party at Judge Armstrong's house? That Peruvian bastard."

"He was an Argentinean bastard."

"Well, whatever he was, he had his eyes down your blouse."

"There isn't all that much to see down my blouse, Stu. I shouldn't have to tell *you* that, of all people."

"How many times did you slow dance with him?"

"Twice."

"Oh, bullshit, Pamela. Don't make it worse by lying about it."

I just let them go. I doubted they even noticed. I grabbed fresh clothes and repaired to the shower. When I came out, I was ready to go.

Stu wasn't on the couch.

Then I heard a moaning sound.

I turned. They were on the bed. They were under the covers and I do believe he was inside her, the noises she was making.

But she was still able to look around his arm at me and say, "We made up, McCain. He told me he'd never be jealous again."

"Good for you, Stu."

I'm not sure Stu was hearing much at

the moment. He just sort of continued to work away down there.

"So tonight Stu'll make you a steak," she said around his arm again. And then: "Oh, by the way, Judge Whitney called for you last night. You better call her."

"God, honey, can't you pay a little attention to *me?*"

"Oh, Stu," she said, eradicating my existence. "Oh, Stu Stu Stu." And giggled giggled giggled.

At the office, I called Judge Whitney in her chambers.

"My God, Pamela had nerve enough to come back to town?"

"Surprised me, too."

"And Stu?"

"Yep."

"Well, at least when my family had to endure a scandal, we went as far away as we could. All the way out here. And we never went back to our little town, either. But people these days — well, they're staying at your apartment and probably having a great old time."

"Sure sounded like it when I left this morning."

"Spare me the details, McCain. I have tender ears." Then: "Tish Hardin called me late last night from the hospital."

"Is she sick?"

"She isn't. But her husband Mike is. He sat in a steaming hot bath last night and slashed his wrists. She got him to the hospital and took him in the back way. She's afraid that this'll make people think he killed that Hastings woman."

"Under the circumstances, I'd have to say that that would cross *my* mind, too."

"He's at St. Mallory's. Go see him, talk to him."

"I doubt he'll talk to me."

"It's important that you at least try."

"Let me check my mail and my calls. I'll get over there as soon as I can."

"I'm due in court in ten minutes, McCain. Call me later on this morning. After eleven."

"All right."

"And McCain?"

"Yes?"

"I think you should marry Mary Travers."

I laughed. "What brought that on?"

"Well, everybody in town knows what's happened to her. And everybody also knows that she's still in love with you. She's a very sweet girl."

"I didn't know you gave advice on romance."

"You should know by now, McCain, that I give advice on anything I feel like."

She hung up.

THIRTEEN

He was on the top floor in a cul-de-sac, the nearest room half a hallway distant. A nurse had just stuck a thermometer in his mouth as I walked in. The white room gleamed with sunlight. A wall-mounted TV was muted. The image was that of Garry Moore, a comforting image.

He gave me a little nod. The nurse gave me a nod, too. She was old and tough and serious, the master sergeant type. He looked like Mike Hardin. He didn't even look pale. Both his wrists were bandaged pretty good, though.

I lighted a cigarette and walked over to the window and looked out on the town. In the daylight it's Norman Rockwell. For all its foibles and shortcomings, it's a good town with good people. The exceptions to the latter generally don't bother you with anything worse than brief bursts of malicious gossip or pontification. You could see the changes, though. Like the shopping center distant on the north edge of town. The downtown merchants were scared of it, and rightly so. We had recently added a McDonald's near the community college. There was talk of a pizza chain coming here next year. And then there were the commuters who lived in the large, expensive housing development to the west. Four bedrooms, three baths, two-and-three stall garages. The Interstate would swing by here in another couple years and the number of commuters would triple after that. Judging by things they wrote in the newspaper letter columns, they seem to regard us and our customs as "quaint." Some of the quaintness irritated them. They especially hated farm smells and slow traffic when they were trying to get to their jobs in the morning. I don't believe that a Jaguar or a Mercedes-Benz had ever so much as passed through our little town till the high-powered executives arrived. It was the brave new world of 1962.

After the nurse squeaked out the door, Hardin jammed a cigarette between his lips, fired it up with an expensive lighter, and said, "Pretty stupid, huh?" He held up his wrists to show me. He held them up the way he would little kittens.

"Pretty stupid." We still didn't like each

other but this was no time to play tough guy.

"I can tell you what everybody's saying."

"That you killed her and her brother and then tried to kill yourself rather than face prison."

"Yup. 'Former University Football Star Murders Mistress.'"

"You should write headlines for a living."

He smiled. It was a wide and deep and sincere smile, too. The suicide attempt had transformed him into a relaxed, friendly human being. "I'll have to consider that since I'm soon going to be broke. If not behind bars."

"You kill her?"

We watched each other for a while. Just watched. No particular expressions. Then he glanced out the window and back at me.

"I was always kind of an asshole to you, wasn't I, McCain?"

"Me and a lot of other people, though this probably isn't the time to say it."

"I'm going to be changing that. Or trying, anyway. My wife's only going to stick with me if I try. I wasn't a hell of a lot better with her than anybody else. And the worst thing is that I've been that way pretty much all my life. I knew it, too. And I didn't care. I don't know that my two boys'll ever forgive me." Then: "You think I killed her?"

"Nope."

"How come?"

I shrugged. "Just don't is all. Couldn't tell you why. Just a sense I got."

"Do you usually guess right?"

"About twenty percent of the time."

He laughed. Then gave me a full rich phlegmy minute of a cigarette cough. He said, "I didn't kill her. I sure thought about it when her brother started shaking me down, though."

"He was shaking you down?"

"Nobody told you?"

"No."

"Hell, he was shaking *all* of us down. I got pretty mad and threw him around one night."

"When was this?"

"Two weeks ago."

"You talk to Karen Hastings about it?"

"Yeah. She got real mad. Or pretended to, anyway. Told me how much she hated her brother. How she'd traveled with him with his magic act. He'd do the divorce detective routine. Get her in bed with some rich old bastard, hide behind the curtains

184

and take snapshots of them. And then sell the pictures to the guy for a lot of money. She was honest enough to say that she hadn't minded living that way for several years but then she just wanted out. That's when we met her. That's why she agreed to the setup we had. She thought it would get her away from her brother."

"He told me he couldn't find her."

"Bullshit. He's been out here from day one. She said he had a lot of nasty things going on the side in Chicago but that when he'd run out of money, he came back here and got some from her. Then recently he got the idea of shaking all of us down. Murdoch tells me the little guy hired you?"

"He told me he wanted me to deliver a package. To a woman. That's all he told me."

"You ever deliver it to her?"

"She was dead before I got to her."

He lay his head back on the pillow. For the first time he looked like a sick man. Drained. Weak. "I don't think my life was supposed to turn out this way. I was always supposed to be the hero. The good-looking football star. Now I'll be a creep to everybody."

"Maybe not to the people who matter to you."

He smiled. "You gonna go 'Dear Abby' on me, McCain?"

"Nah. It's too early in the day for that. I only go 'Dear Abby' after a couple of beers."

I was in court for two hours. My client had been charged with shoplifting. He was seventy-six years old.

Judge Frank Clemmons said, "Sid, what the hell're we going to do with you?"

There were only four people in the pews. One of them gasped when Clemmons, who was nearly as old as Sid Cosgrove, said "hell" in court. The other three laughed. Clemmons fixed them with the evil eye.

"Sid, now I've looked into your Army pension and your social security and your savings account and for the life of me I can't figure out why you shoplift. You're not rich but you're set up pretty good. You don't have any reason at all to shoplift. Now the first three times you got caught, I'm told that the store just let you make restitution. But you know how Ken Potter is, especially when he's having a bad day with his rheumatism. Well, looks like you caught him on one of them bad days, Sid, because here you are in court. Now what've you got to say for yourself?"

"I just like to have a little fun."

"That's your defense? That you like to have a little fun?"

"Sure. I sit out to the danged nursing home all day with nothin' to do. So every once in a while I walk into town and have myself a little fun. They all know I shoplift by now. So it's even more fun. See if I can grab somethin' without them catchin' me."

"Well, you've been caught four times. That's not a very good record."

"Yeah, but it gives us all somethin' to talk about at suppertime. Instead of hearin' the same war stories over and over again. Or lookin' at pitchers of everybody's grandkids or great-grandkids. Or listenin' to everybody bitch about their aches and pains. We're old — seems logical that we'd have aches and pains. What's the point in complainin' about 'em?"

"So you shoplift to sort of entertain yourself?"

"Most fun I've had in years. People see how old I am and they expect me to fall over dead any minute. So it's fun to show 'em I've still got the stuff."

Sid made a pretty good case for himself. It was a pretty unique defense and you could see that Judge Clemmons was enjoying himself except when he looked out and saw Ken Potter the dime store owner glaring at him. I would say in fact that Sid was well on his way to becoming a folk hero except that he blew it by falling asleep right then and there. Just dropped off to slumberland with no warning. And talk about your wall-rattling snoring. Folk heroes aren't supposed to do that. And it says so very plainly in the folk hero book of rules. At least it did last time I looked.

I was standing on the courthouse steps, Sid's niece having taken him back to the rest home, when a voice behind me said, "I would've put him in jail."

"Sure you would've," I said when she stood next to me.

"At least for seventy-two hours."

"Sure you would've."

"Well, at least forty-eight."

"Not even twenty-four."

"What makes you so sure?"

"First of all, the jail wouldn't know what to do with anybody that old. And second of all, even as mean as you can get, you're not that mean. Well, not usually."

She gave me one of her rare smiles. She was an undisclosed fifty-something. And still a damned good-looking woman. Hand-tailored business suits, white scarves at the neck, dark hose, one-inch heels, just a touch of gold at the wrist. Standard operating gear for Judge Esme Anne Whitney. All the attire bought, of course, in New York City, which she escaped to three or four times a year.

The day was so ridiculously gorgeous I wanted to run around in circles and give out with Indian whoops. Like a little kid. Maybe roll around in piles of autumn leaves. And then later carve out a jack o'lantern.

"They're all friends of mine and they're all ruined," she said.

"Yeah. I know."

"I talked to Peter Carlson earlier today. He seems to think that when they find the killer that this'll start to fade. I felt very sorry for him. But they were so stupid. This was like some fraternity boy prank or something. Keeping a woman, the four of them. My God." She shook her sculpted head. Great graying hair cut short to emphasize the features of her face. "I know this'll sound pompous, McCain. But I want to help our little town. If you've seen any of the state papers, we're the laughingstock. 'Peyton Place Comes to Iowa.' We don't deserve that." She gave me a second rare smile. "Believe it or not, I realized when I saw all those nasty innuendos in the papers that I love this little town. It's not very sophisticated and there isn't much to do and the Sykeses haven't spent a dime on anything remotely resembling culture — but the people are decent and the town's a nice, safe place to live."

I looked at her and laughed. "Why, Anne Esme Whitney, I can't believe it. You're actually sentimental about our little town here."

Then she did it. Dipped into the small slash pocket of her custom-tailored suit and pulled out a rubber band. I wasn't quick enough. She got me on the nose. She loved shooting rubber bands at me, the way Sid liked shoplifting I suppose. Made me really look forward to my own years of senility.

"It's up to you, McCain."

"To me? What's up to me?"

"To find the killer and get this part of it over with at least."

"Believe me, I'm trying."

"I'm going to say something and you'll probably disagree with me. But at least think about it for a while."

"Fair enough."

"I don't think any of them killed her."

"I'm going to surprise you and say that I agree with you."

"Why, McCain, you're much smarter than I ever realized."

I tapped out a smoke from the pack. "No matter how I think it through, I can't see any of them doing it. They had too much to lose. Even though each one of them is trying to convince me that one of the others did it."

"Crime of passion?"

"Possibly. But only with Karen Hastings. Killing the brother had to be premeditated."

"So that leaves us with whom?"

"Somebody who wanted to destroy them by forcing the whole thing out in the open. Not only destroy their reputations but implicate them in a murder besides. That leaves us with the wives of the four men and a mysterious man in a black Corvette."

"Where he does he fit in?"

"He visited Karen Hastings a number of times recently, I'm told. From the insignia on his license plate, I take it he's an MD."

"Keep me posted, McCain."

"I will."

FOURTEEN

The doctor's name was Ned Evans. His office was out on First Avenue, the main drag in Cedar Rapids. Every once in a while you'd see an interurban track shining through the bricks. Somewhere in this area was the last of the blacksmith barns. Cedar Rapids had always been a special place for me because it was there I got to shake hands with Hopalong Cassidy. He was the most Irish man I'd ever seen except for my cousin Donald, who came here from County Cork. In his black outfit and big dramatic black hat, Hoppy looked like somebody from a different species. Everybody else looked small and incompetent compared to him.

The small city shone like a trophy in the early afternoon sun. I stopped at a drive-in for lunch. The carhops didn't wear roller skates. Penny loafers seemed to be the general choice in shoes. I heard four or five girl-group songs. There was a guy named Phil Spector, a record producer, and that was his specialty, girl groups, wondrous girl groups, and they were so good that when you heard them sing you almost resented it when the following song was sung by a guy. Man, their sounds were so sweet and light and melancholy, they just took you out of reality.

I listened to the radio while I ate. There still hadn't been any response from Russia, though its ships could be seen heading toward Cuba. President Kennedy had called a news conference and then an hour later canceled it. I spent a few minutes with mutant dreams. All those drive-in movie images of radioactive beasts that had formerly been men. I always felt sorry for the mutants. They hadn't asked to be mutants. But that's the way life was. Some of us got the hero roles and the rest of us got to be the ragged, smelly, bulge-eyed mutants. Guess which of us got the women.

The office was in a new two-story building of glass and metal. Very futuristic, like something on the covers of one of my old science fiction magazines. Most of the cars in the parking lot were new. With their huge fins they looked futuristic, too. I always wanted to be one of those guys on science fiction paperback covers. Very tense in their futuristic clothes, a ray gun in their hand, and a lovely scantily clad blonde accompanying them. Just give me a time machine and say goodbye.

Evans's receptionist was young and dark-haired and pretty. She was also competent. While she was taking notes from the phone — lab results, I guessed, given some of the information she was repeating — she inserted a form onto a clipboard and handed it to me along with a pencil. She nodded to an empty chair across the room.

I took the clipboard and went over and sat down. I'd have to wait till she was off the phone to explain that I wasn't here to have my throat examined. I was here to ask the good doctor some questions. I went through a pile of magazines. At least four of them had Khrushchev's photo on the cover.

It was a noisy waiting room thanks to all the toddlers. They crawled, ran, fell down, bumped into things, cried, screamed, laughed, and screamed some more. Their mothers scolded, pleaded, begged, scolded and sighed. Deep, long sighs. Deep, long maternal sighs. They'd earned their sighs.

A nurse took me back to a small office that was crowded with too much office furniture of the wooden variety, too many medical tomes and too many samples of medicine. It was like one of those tiny closets Shemp, Mo, and Larry always found themselves in. Turn around and you give the guy next to you a concussion. The west wall was covered with framed photos of Evans and his family, two pig-tailed teenage girls, and an appealing outdoorsy sort of wife.

Dr. Ned Evans was as advertised by the stewardess I'd talked to earlier. A short, trim, bald man imposing not because of good looks but because in a completely modest way he exuded virility. He had to have been an athlete and a good one. A college wrestler, perhaps.

He wore the white smock over his slacks. A stethoscope sagged around his neck like a tired snake. He held up my card and smiled. "A private investigator. I sure never thought I'd ever have one of you guys in my office." He sat down. "I can give you five minutes. Then I've got to get back to the grind. The flu season is starting early this year."

"Then I'll get right to it. Karen Hastings."

He nodded. He put his hands on the desk. They were big hands and now they were tightening into fists. "I was sleeping

195

with Karen Hastings for three, four months. She'd been a patient of mine. There was a lot of cancer in her family. She was something of a hypochondriac. She came in with a mole she was very worried about. Basal cell carcinoma. I had it biopsied — state law if you take anything off — and we found out it was nothing to be worried about. Most basal cell carcinomas don't spread or metastasize. They stay pretty much where they are and never become anything to worry about. That's how it started. Then one day I was downtown for a quick sandwich and I ran into her. We had a Coke. Three nights later I was sleeping with her. I probably would still be sleeping with her if her brother hadn't started blackmailing me. He'd taken photos of me entering and leaving her place. Then he got a couple of shots of me taking her into a roadhouse. It was the usual bullshit. He'd mail them to my wife if I didn't pay him."

"How much?"

"Three grand."

"Did you pay him?"

"Did I have any choice?"

"Did you keep on seeing her after that?"

"Are you kidding? I figured she was part of it."

"When was the last time you talked to her?"

He thought a moment. "Week ago. She called to say how sorry she was about her brother. That she hadn't had anything to do with the blackmail. She wanted me to come over and see her. She said she was in love with me."

"Did you believe that?"

"No. Or at least I didn't care if she was telling me the truth."

"Why's that?"

He made a face. "Why's that? Well, I'm forty-four years old, I have an enviable medical practice, my peers tell me I'm damned good at what I do — and most of all I've got a wife and two daughters I love more than anything on this earth. And when I finally woke up and realized that I was jeopardizing it all — I just wanted out."

"He would've kept blackmailing you."

"I know."

"That's a pretty good reason for killing somebody."

"I know that, too. Ever since I heard about her being killed — and then him on top of it — I can't relax. I have to force myself to concentrate on my work. I just keep waiting for the knock on the door.

The police. I'll be a murder suspect and it'll all come out and I'll be ruined. Like those four stupid bastards who put up the money for her."

"Why 'stupid'?"

"Are you kidding? How long did they think before it'd get out?"

"You spent time with her."

"Yeah, but I didn't put her on the payroll." Then: "Whether you noticed it or not, I'm scared shitless."

It was one of those moments when somebody sort of forces you to like them against your better judgment.

"She was beautiful," he said, "and I'd never had sex like that. Never once. Hell, I wasn't even attractive to women until I got in my forties. I think it's being bald. I'm not kidding you. I lose my hair, women suddenly start showing interest in me. I was always the best friend, the blind date, the guy who couldn't get to first base when everybody else was hitting home runs. And then I lose my hair and women seem to like me."

"Maybe it's the 'vette."

"I've thought of that, believe me. Or maybe it's the combination." He covered his face with his hands and took several deep breaths. A relaxing technique. He took his hands away and said, "Think the police'll find out about me?"

"I don't know. But I'd get a lawyer right away."

"Are you serious?"

"Yeah. Right now this thing is spinning out of control. Not everybody was playing by the rules. She was seeing you and maybe a few others besides her benefactors. So I wouldn't be surprised if a few more names get tossed into the ring. But I'd get a lawyer. I'd prepare for the worst."

"If I can prove I didn't kill her will my name come out?"

"In other words, can you make a deal with the cops? Probably. As long as you've got a damned good alibi. I think they can arrange to keep it quiet."

"I was at a county medical board meeting the whole night. Then we ended up at this after-hours place. Sort of a dive. And I was with another doctor the whole time. Paul Kendrick. He had the car. I rode with him. I couldn't have slipped away even if I'd wanted to."

"Kendrick'll vouch for you?"

"I'll call him right now if you want me to."

"I'll take your word for it. The cops won't." Then: "One final thing. You ever see her upset — afraid, angry, anything like that — and couldn't figure out why?"

He leaned back and gave it some thought. "Once, I guess. She kept looking out the window. She seemed agitated about something. I had the sense somebody was out there."

"In a car, you mean?"

"I'm not sure. It's just — she kept looking out the window and then she'd be very uptight for a while. Chewing her lip. Not paying attention to what I was saying. Chain smoking. I'd never seen her act that way."

"Did you have any sense of her life outside of you?"

"That was the funny thing. No, I didn't. She never mentioned another person or a job or even what she liked to do. And she was more worried about people seeing us out and about than I was. I'd ask her about it of course but she'd just laugh and say 'I'm a mystery woman.' And she wasn't kidding." A glance at the wrist watch. "I really should call a lawyer?"

I said, "You really should call a lawyer."

I sat in my car with a Pepsi and some smokes listening to Ross Murdoch's press conference. He made a brief statement announcing his resignation for "personal reasons" and said that he was very sorry for what this would do to his political party. He said he would take no questions and he meant it. He had already put a prominent criminal defense lawyer named Richard Spellman on the payroll. He was from Chicago and he was good. Spellman took the questions. I'd just heard the national news a few minutes earlier. Still no word from Russia. But their ships had yet to turn back. They were still churning toward the distant blockade.

I'd come out to the now-closed park for a long walk. The Murdoch story was so lurid that it had become more interesting to locals than the possibility of nuclear war.

I looked out at the river below. The last of the autumn's motor boats raced up and down the blue water. The birches on the far shore looked white and clean and pure. Staggered up the hill were oaks and maples, peacock-splendid in their colors.

I shut off the radio and got out of the car for my walk. I took my pocket-sized spiral notebook along, flipping back through my notes as I went. I still hadn't interviewed Peter Carlson, which I wasn't looking forward to. I wasn't sure I could even get to him. He would have hired a smart lawyer by now.

I walked 'till dusk. The cornfields were a dirty golden color now that the crop had been picked, the stalks like fallen soldiers.

On the drive back to town I thought about Mary and Pamela. My folks' generation was the last to be dutiful mates. My generation was already setting records for divorces. Innumerable sociologists had already written innumerable tomes on the subject. I suppose it had something to do with how a lot of us had been raised. Virtually everything in our lives was disposable. Very little lasted very long — certainly not our cars, our appliances, our homes. So we got new ones. Why should spouses be any different? There were plenty of those around, too.

On the way home, because of a commercial on the radio, I figured out how Karen Hastings' body might have been carried into Ross Murdoch's house.

"You like?" Stu said.

He wore an apron that said Master Chef on it. It had a silly suburban face right below the script. You throw everything in a suitcase as you make a desperate trip to find your gone-fled wife and you make sure to pack your Master Chef apron?

"Doesn't Stu sound Chinese when he says that?" Pamela laughed.

"Oh, yes, very Chinese," I said.

" 'You like?' " she said. "He's so cute."

"Downright adorable," I said.

"So you haven't told me, Sam," Stu said, seating himself. "How's the steak?"

"Great." And it was. Stu truly was a Master Chef.

We were eating steaks on my wobbly dining room table. Stu was playing a Pat Boone album — my God, he must've packed that, too — and Pamela was wearing some kind of Kabuki robe. Stu spoke Chinese and she wore Kabuki. An international couple.

"We're really starting to like your little apartment," Stu said. "I haven't lived in a place like this since college. I had a little more room and it was a little nicer but this is growing on me."

"Growing," I said.

"Stu is even getting used to the kitty litter box."

"It's pretty darned unsanitary," he said, "when you come right down to it. But I want to keep my pumpkin happy. She loves cats. I'm a dog man, myself. They go outside when they want to go number two.

Well, or number one for that matter."

"In case you haven't noticed," Pamela said, "we've decided to stay married."

"Gee," I said, "there's good news."

"We're going to buy a new house when we get back to Chicago."

"And a new car."

"We owe you a lot, Sam," Stu said, "you know, letting us stay in your little apartment like this."

Pamela smiled. "Even with the kitty litter, hon?" She had pieces of steak in her teeth.

Stu was one of those guys — like Red Skelton — who always signaled when he was about to tell a joke. He laughed right before delivering it. "You know what I told Pumpkin here — I'm just glad *I* don't have to use a kitty litter box when I want to go to the bathroom."

Pamela covered her mouth with a napkin, she was laughing so hard. "God, what a picture that would make. Stu and a kitty litter box."

"I really do enjoy it here in your little apartment," Stu said. "It really is just like being back in college again."

"Same with me, Sam. I took a bubble bath this afternoon. I stayed in there for two hours. Nobody knows we're here. It's sort of like hiding out."

"Yes," Stu said, "that's it exactly, honey. It's like that Bogie movie we love. 'High Sahara.' "

I said, "I think that's 'Sierra.' "

"Pardon?" said Stu the Master Chef.

"I think it's 'High Sierra.' Not 'High Sahara.' It's set in the Sierra mountains."

He had a mouthful of steak. He jabbed his fork in my direction, "You know what, honey? You never told me that this guy knows movie titles the way he does. He's great."

The phone rang. I damned near leaped over the couch to get it. Whoever it was, I was visiting them. Or at least saying I was.

Deirdre said, "Could you come out to the house, Sam? Dad's lawyer would like to talk with you. He's pretty sure Cliffie's getting ready to arrest Dad. God, I can't believe this is happening."

"I'll be there in five minutes."

"Are you sure I'm not interrupting anything?"

"Nothing I'd care to talk about."

I went back to the table. "I need to get out of here. I'll throw some stuff in my gym bag. Take my clothes along for tomorrow. You folks have any idea when you might be leaving?"

"Well, as I said, Sam," the Master Chef said, "we're really starting to relax finally. We thought we'd talk to our respective parents tomorrow and then see how a few of our respective old friends felt about getting together for a few drinks. You know, sort of ease ourselves back into society, if you will."

"So we're talking what here?"

They looked at each other and then at me.

The master chefette said, "Well, we'll try to find a place to stay but if we can't — I don't think we're talking more than four or five days to stay here. I mean, even after we see everybody, we can still hide out. Nobody would ever expect us to be in a place like this."

Nuclear holocaust was sounding better all the time.

FIFTEEN

He was fleshy but imposing, a hint of revered Roman senator in the stark outsize features and coiled white hair. The extra weight added some years to him but the added years helped. Spellman, his name was. Richard Spellman. He had one brother who was a senator and another brother who was a Catholic bishop. Not to be confused with the cardinal.

He perched on the edge of Ross Murdoch's desk. He wore a black crewneck sweater, blue jeans, white socks, shiny black loafers with tassels. Tassels on men's shoes have always irritated me. This is one of the possible reasons they keep me up here on the violent ward. Ritz crackers have been known to send me into seizures. Then there was the day I jumped up on the table and denounced waxed paper. Other than that I can keep myself under control. Pretty much.

He had a cigarette in one hand, a social

glass of sherry in the other. I'd declined the sherry. I'd spent twenty minutes bringing him up to date. "You going to be threatened when I bring in my own detective?"

"Not at all," I said. Which was what I was supposed to say. Nobody likes to be second-guessed. But everybody has to pretend they don't mind it. *Your man exposing me as a complete bumbling incompetent fool? Now why would I mind that, Mr. Spellman?*

"As I see it," he went on, "we have two problems. One, we need to find out how she was brought in here. A body isn't all that easy to disguise. And two, we need to find out who had the strongest motive to kill her. Of the four men involved, I mean."

"So you're assuming that it was one of the four who were paying her rent?" I said.

"I don't eliminate anything, McCain. But I'll tell you, to me this is like a husband finding a wife dead. The automatic suspect to the coppers is the husband. Big city or small town doesn't make any difference. That's who the coppers look at initially and you have a hell of a time moving away from that position."

"Have you eliminated me, Dick?" Murdoch said, trying to sound droll.

"Of course not, Ross. Don't take it personally. But I've only been working with you for the past five hours. I haven't had time to form any opinions about anything yet except that your chief-of-police is a baboon."

"You talked to Cliffie?" I said.

"Courtesy call," Spellman said, draining his sherry glass and setting it down. "Sonofabitch is sitting in his office reading a comic book. Donald Duck. I still read Batman once in a while, you know, kind've for old times sake. But Donald Duck? At our age? Anyway, so I introduce myself, being very courteous and all, knowing I'll have to work with this dipshit for the foreseeable future, and you know what? He won't shake my hand. I put my hand out there. And he won't shake it. You know what he says to me? 'I don't shake hands with men who work for killers.' I'm still polite, of course, and I say, 'If you mean Ross Murdoch, do you have any solid evidence?' And he says what I expect him to say, 'lady is found in his bomb shelter, what more evidence do you want?' And so on. Then he tells me he's busy and he needs get back to work. And then you know what? I'm walking down the hall away from his office, heading for the front door, right? And I hear him laughing. And he says 'Oh, that Gyro Gearloose.' Gyro Gearloose? And this chief of yours is supposed to be a grown-up?"

"I still like Gyro Gearloose," I said. "Carl Barks is the great guy who writes and draws him."

He gave me an odd look. "I wouldn't spread that around if I were you." He wasn't kidding. Then: "You'll be happy to know, Ross, that I'm actually going on the assumption that you didn't kill her."

"I appreciate that."

"But your man McCain here has given me some pretty good motives to work with, I mean."

Your Man McCain? A possible TV series? —

"I haven't seen those," Murdoch said, nodding at the notebook in Spellman's hand.

"This Carlson — he was jealous of her? Having to share her?"

"Yes."

"This Mike Hardin — he loses all his money. He could have been forced into killing her because he was broke and didn't want you people to know."

"How about Gavin Wheeler?"

"He doesn't have anything written down here."

I sat up straighter in my chair. The way you do when the nun calls on you for the answer to the question she just asked that you in your daydreaming didn't hear.

"He's just an all-around jerk," I said. To Murdoch, I said, "Did Carlson really try and buy up all your shares?"

"Yes," Murdoch said. "He wanted her for himself."

"Did she want him?"

"He's the only one who can answer that," Murdoch said.

"So there's nothing with Gavin Wheeler?" Spellman said. He was not a patient man.

"Nothing specific," I said. "But I guess I could see him killing somebody."

"Maybe he could kill Gyro Gearloose for me."

I'm glad Ross-about-to-be-arrested-for-murder found Spellman so funny.

I decided to trump him. "I may have figured out how her body got in here."

"You're kidding," Spellman said.

"There's a new rug in the bomb shelter. I don't know if anybody gave it any thought, any law enforcement people. Ross, do you happen to know when it was delivered?"

"I'd have to check to be sure. But I guess it would have been the afternoon before I found Karen in the bomb shelter."

"It's a long shot," Spellman said.

"True," I said, "but right now we have to consider it a possibility. Who'd you buy it from?"

"Home Furnishings. I always try to buy everything I can in town here. You know, support the town. Our merchants are getting massacred by the shopping center and with Cedar Rapids and Iowa City so near. I gave my ladies strict orders to buy whatever they could right here."

I tried to imagine giving Deirdre Murdoch a strict order. It wasn't easy. She just wasn't a strict-order kind of girl.

"I'll get the name of the driver and talk to him," I said.

"The toughest part of this'll be getting the names of enemies she made before she came here," Spellman said. "She played a rough game. Even when you're a high-priced call-girl — which in essence is what she was — it's still a dangerous job. You run into some real nut jobs. They fall in love with you, they follow you, they get scared they're going to be found out, they're woman-haters deep down — you've got all these things in play."

"And then you start shaking them down," I said.

"Exactly," Spellman said. "You start shaking them down. And that's when they get really dangerous. You may have let something slip that makes you especially dangerous. It's not just getting your time with her exposed — maybe she knows something that can send the guy to prison. He panics. He can't spend the rest of his life worrying that every day might be the day she hands you over to some DA somewhere in order to save her own skin."

"So he kills her," I said. "And her brother, too. The killer figuring the brother probably knows his secret also."

"Good Lord," Ross Murdoch said. "If that's the case, the killer could have been in town a couple of hours and then gone back home to wherever he lives."

"It's possible."

"I still think it was local," I said.

"You don't, of course, have any proof of that?"

"No, I don't. But being a good defense lawyer, I'll make some up if you'll give me a couple of minutes."

"I love working with people who're strictly local," Spellman said. He sounded weary and long-suffering. I was beginning to suspect that deep down I didn't like this guy. As in I'd like to run him down with my ragtop and then back over him a few times.

"And I love working with people who waste time overlooking the obvious." I looked at Ross. "Karen Hastings and her brother were shaking you and your friends down for more money. And then they both wind up dead, one of them in your bomb shelter. Does any of this sound like somebody who just happened to be breezing through town?"

"He makes some good points," Murdoch said.

Spellman was saved from responding because the phone rang.

Murdoch picked up, listened and said, "Thank you." He hung up again. "I have a friend in the police department. His father worked for me for years. He just wanted to warn me that Sykes is on his way to arrest me." He glanced at me and said, "I'm going to wait for him on the porch."

"Why the hell would you do that?"

He would do that because he knew the kind of mischief Cliffie would be up to.

Three police cars arrived, sweeping up the drive. One had its red lights going. No siren, at least. Cliffie was restraining himself in his old age.

And then came the press. Cliffie had apparently invited every reporter in a six-state area. There was, and I do not exaggerate, a caravan of at least fifteen cars, station wagons and vans.

A low fog had set in. The reporters hit the front lawn like soldiers on a beach landing. They resembled monsters. The fog cut them off at the waist. They all moved toward a single place — the center of the front porch on which Ross Murdoch stood in his top coat with the brim of his grey dress hat pulled low over his face.

Murdoch knew how Cliffie operated. If Murdoch hadn't been on his porch, Cliffie would've walked in a crouch up to the front door, his gun drawn, waving to his men to fan out, as if Murdoch was going to come charging through the front doors with a couple of grenade launchers and an armload of automatic weapons. Murdoch had just decided to deprive Cliffie of his usual fun. Cliffie would pistol-whip a nun if he thought there was a press camera nearby. And then explain why the eighty-two-year-old Sister was a true danger to the community.

Cliffie kept looking over his shoulder. There weren't any live TV cameras, just three youths with bad complexions holding shaky film cameras. The film would be bathed in time for the ten o'clock news.

When he was sure that the cameras were rolling, Cliffie said, "Ross Murdoch I arrest you on the charge of first degree murder."

"Oh, for God's sake, Cliffie, cut the cornball bullshit," I said.

The cameras swung to me. "He knows he's being arrested. He's been standing here for fifteen minutes waiting for you to arrest him. And he's obviously going to go along peacefully. And he has nothing to say at this point except that these charges are ridiculous, as does his lawyer, the famous Richard Spellman from Chicago." I nodded to Spellman. "Mr. Spellman, if you would."

This was all happening too quickly for Cliffie. He was getting whiplash from gaping around so much. All he knew for sure was that he wasn't the center of attention any more. And here he'd dressed up so well for the occasion, too. Cliffie secretly thinks he's Glenn Ford. I can't put that down, because I secretly think I'm Robert Ryan. Cliffie's too chunky and ugly to be Ford and as I've remarked elsewhere, except for the height, the good looks, the voice and manly poise, I'm pretty much a dead ringer for Robert Ryan.

Cliffie stood hip-cocked with his hand resting on the butt of his gun. The way he sneered at Spellman made me think Spellman wasn't such a bad sort, after all.

"There's no doubt that Mr. Murdoch has done some things that he truly regrets," Spellman said to the battery of microphones pointed at him. And that was a good strategy. Get the kept-woman problem out of the way up front. "He's a decent man and admits that he feels shame for some of his conduct and for the grief he's brought to his family. His days as a public man are over. He's already stepped out of the race for governor.

"But what we're talking about here is an error — and a major one — in moral judgment. But we are not — and let me repeat *are not* — talking about murder. He did not murder Karen Hastings nor did he have anything to do with putting her body in his bomb shelter. It is clear to me that the real killer managed to secrete the body inside Mr. Murdoch's home. I have no idea how this happened. But with the help of my investigators — and one of your own local investigators, Mr. Sam McCain, who has already been extremely helpful to our investigation — we're going to clear Mr. Murdoch's name long before this matter is brought to trial. And that's a promise."

He had no more paused for breath than the reporters began shouting questions at him.

"The blonde woman in the blue hat asked me what about the other three men involved in this. And I can't speak to that. I haven't been asked to represent them and I'd imagine they'll each want their own lawyers — if there are even any charges. Again, the arrangement they had with the Hastings woman was morally indefensible but it doesn't seem to me that any laws were broken. Police Chief Sykes has chosen to arrest my client, and it's my client I'm concerned about. I'm sure Chief Sykes would be happy to answer your questions."

I was standing next to Spellman. When the cameras and microphones swooped over to Cliffie, Spellman said, "Cliffie'll probably tell them about the time he had a gunfight with Jesse James." He looked at all the reporters. "This guy should be a campaign manager. He can really get the press to turn out." Then he smiled at me. "Sorry we got off to a bad start inside. I can be a bit of a prima donna. But the next time I express my true and profound love for myself and all my sage opinions, remind me that I grew up in Groverton, Illinois, population eight hundred and seventy-two. That always keeps me humble."

I smiled. "Thanks for the plug. I can use the business."

"Could you meet me at Murdoch's office tomorrow morning at nine? I always like to review things. You can meet my guy from Chicago."

"See you then."

Then Deirdre came through the front door and said, "Sam, could you come inside a minute, please?"

Spellman winked at me. "I'd come inside that gal any time she asked."

I went up the steps. She stood aside for me and I went inside to the light and warmth and splendor of her home.

We stood in the vestibule. She flipped off the light. "My dad wants my mom to go into the hospital again."

"When did he say this?"

"Earlier tonight. He called and made the arrangement himself. He has a pilot and plane standing by in Cedar Rapids to take her."

"You don't want her to go?"

"I'm just wondering what his thinking is."

I didn't say anything. I wanted her to say it herself.

Outside, Cliffie was still talking. He allowed as how this was a scandal that would probably be picked up everywhere in the country. And because of that, he said, he wanted to bring swift justice to the murderer so that the fine Midwestern folk who lived here could get on with their lives. Never mind that the poor, sensitive folk were enjoying the hell out of this; and never mind that the town would enjoy an economic boost when the trial was in session. There'd be more reporters than citizens. And never mind that the man Cliffie had already convicted was likely the wrong man.

"I think he thinks she did it."

"Your father thinks your mom did it?"

"Yes."

"And that's why he's sending her away."

She pressed herself against me. Her hair smelled sweet and clean from a recent shampoo and she was a marvel of soft flesh and gentle curves. She clung to me the way a child would. But her grip wasn't strong. Weariness had set in. She was fatigued both physically and mentally. She could probably use a hospital stay herself, just to recover from her anxiety and exhaustion.

"I still can't believe this is happening," she said.

"You need some rest."

She leaned away from me. "What if she really did it?"

"There's no answer to that. It's hypothetical. You're reading things into a situation that may be just what it seems to be. I mean, your dad loves your mom and wants her to be healthy. The strain you're all under and her past psychiatric record — this is the best thing, I'm sure."

"You really think it could be that simple?"

"I really do."

She clung to me once more. Cliffie was speaking in an especially loud voice now. He was going into his "morality" speech about how the US of A was such a decadent country these days, the commies wouldn't have a hard time taking us over at all. Hell, we might even *want* them to take over, all of us dancing naked around a huge statue of Khrushchev, as the pagan fires burned higher and higher.

The assembled reporters groaned, tittered and a few of the braver ones laughed out loud. Cliffie never sounded dumber than when he tried to save the national soul.

She stepped back from me. "Maybe you're right. Maybe I'm so tired I'm just making things up. Getting really paranoid."

"For now anyway, I'd just let your mother go. Make sure she packs everything she needs and say goodbye. You could always drive her to the airport yourself."

"I'd thought of that, Sam. But what if I'm needed here?"

I took her hand. "I'm going back to work. Your dad's going to jail for a couple of hours, just till Spellman bails him out, and your mother needs a ride. There isn't anything for you to do but sit here and worry. And your mom would appreciate you for taking her rather than one of your dad's staffers."

"No staffers left," she said. "He gave them all very big checks and said goodbye. To the ones who worked here in town, anyway. The other paid staffers will get their checks tomorrow or the next day. Dad feels guilty about letting them down. They worked very hard for him. And then it ended like this. But that's dad's style. He has this sense of guilt and when that takes over, he'll give you anything he owns."

"Take your mom, Deirdre. She'll appreciate it and it'll get you out of this house."

"It still seems unreal, Sam."

"That's how these things go. Most people never experience this side of the law. And it's scary when you realize that even if you're a powerful man — like your father — that an incompetent like Cliffie can completely take your life over and make you jump through any kind of hoops he puts up for you. Then think of what it'd be like if you didn't have any money or power at all. No bail. If you've got an honest cop, an honest judge and a fair-minded jury pool — and you're innocent — you've got a fifty-fifty chance of going free." I took her by the shoulders. "Your father's going to go free, Deirdre. The charges'll be dropped."

"You really believe that, Sam."

I really *wanted* to believe it, anyway.

"Yeah, I really do. Now why don't you go help your mother?"

She gave me another one of those exotic erotic fleeting kisses of hers and then hurried toward the grand staircase.

SIXTEEN

THINK WE FOUND A PLACE.
THANKS FOR EVERYTHING.
                    PAMELA

There was quite a party going on at my place. The cats were sitting up on the couch with their legs crossed watching that new Johnny Carson late night show. They were drinking bourbon and smoking cigars. Tess was wearing a party hat I had left over from last New Year's Eve. I'd begun to suspect that they had lives very much like ours. But they tried to keep them secret for fear of my inhibiting them. In my fantasy, the cigars and the bourbon had to do with Pamela and Stu moving out. Far out. They knew, as I knew, that that long malaise known as Heartsick About Pamela In Black River Falls, Iowa had ended. I was over her. I hadn't liked her for many years but I'd loved her. Now I didn't like her or love her. No wonder the cats were whooping it up. The intruders were gone and they wouldn't have to listen to any more love-sick mooning on my part.

Law enforcement people say that they're trained to spot things other people don't notice. I must've been out sick the days they were conducting these courses at the police academy in Des Moines, because I miss things even the blind can see.

Not until I'd gone to the john, checked my service for phone messages, turned up the heat, pulled on a ragged U of Iowa sweatshirt, and sat myself down in my recliner did I notice the imposing round foil-wrapped plate in the center of the table.

I went over and inspected it. Tess was there to help me. She knew, as I did, that it was a plate covered with food. Tess has gone to drama school the past two years. She knows how to look up at you with those large intelligent eyes and make you want to cry. And share. "I'll tell you what. You can have it all if it's anything like liver and broccoli. How's that?" I was thinking that if cats knew how to give you the finger, that's what she would have been doing just then. Cats are smart. They know all about stuff like liver and broccoli.

It was a white meat chicken sandwich with lettuce, tomato and mayo, a small chilled tin of V-8, several carrot sticks and a good hunk of chocolate cake. There was a tiny card that read *From a secret admirer who thinks you're getting too skinny. Mary.* Mrs. Goldman would have let her in. She was one of the many people who thought that Mary and I should've gotten married a long time ago.

I had to keep pushing Tess away. "You can have half the carrot sticks." Oh, yeah; she definitely would've given me the finger if she could.

I ate sitting in the recliner. I then polished off the beer, smoked a few cigarettes and thought about Mary. Looks, smarts, tenderness, laughs. That was Mary. But Mary also offered love so strong it was sometimes overwhelming, smothering. Always had, always would. Just her nature. And now Mary offered two kids in tow as well.

I didn't find the teddy bear until I slid under the covers. A big brown teddy bear wearing a lawman's badge. A tiny note Scotch-taped to it: *Your Secret Admirer.* God, it was corny but there in the wind-whipped prairie night it felt good to know that she was out there, thinking of me.

"Who's this guy?" my dad said at seven-thirty the following morning.

"I don't know. He claims to be our son. He just showed up here a few minutes ago. Says he lived with us for a long time. But I'm not sure we have a son, do we? If we have, I haven't seen him in a long, long time."

"Years and years," Dad said.

"You have any ID?" Mom said, dishing up the pancakes and the bacon and setting it in front of me. The milk and orange juice and daily vitamin were already in front of me on the kitchen table.

"How come he gets to eat first?" Dad said. "We don't even know if he belongs to us."

"Whoever he is, he seems to think he's real important. Says he's got a big meeting at nine and has to be ready for it."

"Yeah, he looks important all right," Dad said.

"Gee, I'm sure glad Abbott and Costello started making movies again," I said.

"So how are you, son?"

"Don't let him off the hook so easily," Mom said. "We don't hear from him for nearly a week, he deserves a little razzing."

Mom and Dad are a matched set. Mom is five-two and most of her hair is still red. Dad is five-six and most of his hair has gone to hair heaven. Toward the end of my high school years, Dad got promoted at the factory where he'd worked since coming back from the war, and for the first time our family moved to a respectable neighborhood, lived in a house and drove a respectable used Ford. My sister Ruth lived in Chicago. She'd moved there after getting pregnant when she was seventeen. Nobody was happy about it but she sure wouldn't get an abortion, not even in sinful Chicago. Even though I thought that was the best solution, my folks were shocked when I even brought it up. She'd have to give prior notice before she came back here so we could give the most important of the gossips plenty of time to work up their most venomous scorn. Sometimes, as now, I'd look across the table and imagine Ruthie still there, that sweet Mick face of freckles and slightly imperious nose and great gladifying lopsided McCain smile. Granddad wore it even in his coffin. Her life had been peaceful and almost perfect until her pregnancy and since then it had been nothing but travail in Chicago — a mother who worked and left her kid at the YMCA center; a number of hopeless, hapless, unhealthy affairs; a boozy slur in the voice when she called sometimes; and a sense I shared with Mom and Dad that she wasn't Ruth any more, not the Ruth we'd known, and that she was as sad about it as we were. But none of us had any idea what to do about it. Sometimes I'd think of her and I swear to God I just wanted to die right on the spot, my entire body and mind in pain — take my gun and put it to my temple and just fire it before I had time to back out of it — it was just so hard to think about how much I loved her and was helpless in the face of her grief and sorrow.

But this was a sunny morning and Captain Kangaroo was on TV in the living room — Mom still watched it because Ruth had always watched it in the morning; I suppose it was a way of keeping her with us — and Mom was saying, "I think they could plead insanity and get away with it."

Around a mouthful of pancake, I said, "Who should plead insanity because they could get away with it?"

"She means Ross Murdoch and those other three. That's all she's been talking about. I keep trying to tell her things like that go on all the time."

"Why, a situation like that is no better than prostitution," Mom said.

Dad said, "That's what you can do when you have money."

Mom said, "You can have your own

geisha woman if you have money is what you're saying? There aren't any *better* things to do than that?"

Dad said, "If you have a lot of money you can do that and *still* do all the other better things, too."

Mom said, "It's their wives I feel sorry for. And their children. My Lord, the gossips will have a field day."

"Already are," I said. "Everywhere I go people tell me Murdoch jokes."

"She must've had some temper," Dad said.

"How's that? And may I have some syrup?"

"You see how polite he is since he moved out of the house?" Mom said.

Dad winked at her, making sure I saw it. "Maybe he should have moved out sooner. He'd be even *more* polite by now."

"Maybe I didn't raise him right," Mom said.

"Oh, Lord," Dad said, "I wish those magazines had never been published."

Mom was a reader of parental magazines. How to train Little Bobby not to poop in his soup; hit the kitties with his hammer; say dirty words to company before he reached the age of three. You know the magazines I'm talking about. Like most women of her generation, Mom spent a number of hours per week perusing these rags and then torturing herself with the certain knowledge that she had failed me as a loving mom, tutor and inspirer of lofty goals.

"So what's this about her temper?"

"Scotty McBain down to the plant?"

"Uh-huh," I said. I was working on the three strips of delicately wrought bacon.

"He said she had some temper."

"Who did?" I said.

"That gal they were keeping."

"Karen Hastings?"

He nodded. He was working on his bacon, too.

"How did Scotty McBain know she had a temper?"

"In the summer he's got this canoe rental deal he runs on the side. His wife works there during the day and then he takes over when he's done at the plant."

"Oh. Right. I forgot."

"Anyway, this Hastings gal, she used to go around with this gal got a trailer right up the road from where Scotty's got his canoe renting deal. Very nice looking gal."

"What're you doing, honey?" Mom asked me.

"Writing."

"Writing what?"

"I'm putting what Dad says in my note-book so I'll remember to follow up on this."

"Are you working on this thing?" Dad said.

"Uh-huh. Go ahead."

Dad shrugged. "Well, it isn't any big deal. This gal — I don't remember her name — and the Hastings gal, they'd rent canoes together, see. And so one day they were climbing into their canoe and a couple guys — smart-asses, you know — started makin' remarks. You know how guys get. And Scotty said they were pretty drunk, besides. He wouldn't rent 'em a canoe. So anyway you got these two really good lookin' gals and these two smart-asses and the gals kinda play along while they're getting their canoe ready and then one of the guys kinda pats the Hastings gal on the rump. And man. Scotty says he never saw a woman hit a man as hard as she did that guy. Really rocked him. And she wasn't much bigger than your mom. Scotty said the guys were really mad but they backed off and left."

"Scotty still working at the plant?"

"Nope. He retired about the time I did."

"I still say I feel sorry for their families,"

Mom said. "And their poor kids."

"Well, most of their kids are grown up by now," I said.

"I hear Murdoch hired a Chicago lawyer, huh?"

"Yep. Very big-time guy. Seems all right."

"He's going to need Perry Mason," Mom said. "That poor woman dead in his bomb shelter."

" 'Poor woman'?," Dad said. "I thought you said she was just a prostitute."

"Well, that doesn't mean anybody had the right to kill her. She could've made a good confession and started her life over again."

My mom is of the belief that everybody is Catholic. Or secretly wants to be. Or should be. Or will be. Someday. If we just wait patiently long enough.

This time, it was me my dad winked at. "What if she was Methodist?"

"Well, she still could've started over. Nobody had the right to kill her."

"Murdoch must have really panicked," Dad said. "Leaving her there in that bomb shelter. Say, is that as fancy as everybody says?"

"The bomb shelter?" I said. "It sure is."

"We're having another prayer vigil tonight," Mom said softly. "I'm just asking God that Khrushchev comes to his senses." She took Dad's hand. He smiled at her. "We've had our lives. It's the children I'm worried about. They should have their chance to live." She looked at me. "You could always come to the vigil tonight, Sam."

"It'd be nice," I said, "if I get the time."

"That means," Dad said, "there's not a chance in hell he's going to be there."

Mom actually smiled. "You think I don't know that?"

I decided to start the meeting with Spellman and his investigator Del Merrick with a shocker. I'd awakened in the middle of the night with an idea we should have considered all along.

"We're assuming that Ross Murdoch didn't murder Karen Hastings," I said.

They both nodded. They looked as if they'd slept in. Spellman even had sleep lines on one side of his face. Merrick was a middle-aged man with rusty-colored hair and a good blue suit.

"That's right," Spellman said. "You're not going to tell me that he killed her, are you? Nobody'd leave a body in his own house like that."

"True — or probably true. Maybe he got into a situation where he killed her and couldn't figure out a way to get rid of the body."

Spellman's face was knitted with irritation. "So you *are* saying he killed her."

"No, I'm just saying let's re-think the assumptions we've made so far. I've made them, too. But I've been thinking about a different way this could have happened."

Spellman said, "Well, let's hear it. No offense, McCain, but we're sitting with the best criminal investigator I've ever worked with. If he thinks it'll fly, then it'll fly."

Merrick actually blushed from the praise. I liked him right away. A modest man. He said, "My old man was a lot better than I was. He went head-to-head with old J. Edgar twice and won both times. Found the killers before Hoover's men did. Hoover kept trying to nail him after that. You didn't embarrass Hoover and get away with it."

I drank some coffee and said, "I don't think Ross Murdoch killed her. I don't think he knew anything about the body until, as he said, he opened the bomb shelter."

"So how did the body get carried inside?" Spellman said.

"That's the assumption I want to knock down. First of all, the entire family was gone the day before the body was discovered. Ross was at a meeting in Des Moines, Mrs. Murdoch was visiting her other sister in Iowa City, and Deirdre was at the hospital here working as a candy-striper."

"A what?" Merrick asked.

"A volunteer. They call them candy-stripers. She was at the hospital from nine in the morning until around six-thirty. Her parents got home just before she did. Their part-time maid had fixed dinner for them. Mrs. Murdoch heated the dinner and they ate together."

"So you're saying somebody brought Karen Hastings's body in while the family was gone?" Spellman said. "They still had to sneak her in past the workmen."

"Nobody snuck her in," I said.

"You're losing me here, McCain. If Ross didn't kill her and nobody snuck the body in, then how did she end up in the bomb shelter?"

"This is the part I should've thought of before. The workers all left at five. That left roughly an hour and a half that the house was empty. This is where we have to start looking at the other three partners in the deal. It wouldn't be difficult for one of them to call Karen and tell her to meet them at Murdoch's place. She'd been wanting to leave town and take a lot of money with her. That would be the lure to get her there. All the caller had to say was that they'd come up with the money and that they'd hand it over."

"Wouldn't she think that meeting at Murdoch's was strange?" Merrick said.

"Not if the caller said that the Murdochs had some kind of dinner or something they had to attend. And that it'd be safe to meet her there."

"So the caller gets her in the house, kills her, leaves her in the bomb shelter," Spellman said, "and Ross Murdoch gets charged with murder."

"That makes more sense than hauling a body past all those workmen," Merrick said. "I didn't like that theory at all. Way too risky. And even if all the other workmen had gone home, there'd be the chance that somebody would see a truck or a car pull in about then. I checked the Murdoch road. A lot of people use it to and from work."

"So one of the three really has something against Murdoch," Spellman said.

"Some old grudge, maybe, that we

haven't learned about yet."

Merrick looked at Spellman. "Sam here knows all the players. I say let's turn him loose on this."

"No offense, Sam, but it's just a theory."

"Still makes more sense," Merrick said, "than hauling a body around. You kill her in one place and then wrap her up and stash her in a car trunk and take her someplace else. A lot of things could go wrong. But if you could get her into the empty house, kill her and leave her there — a lot safer than transporting her all over hell."

"You've saved yourself blackmail money," I said, "and you've turned Ross Murdoch into a murderer. How does he explain a body in his bomb shelter?"

"Cliffie comes and arrests you," Spellman said, "and the entire potential jury pool has already assumed your guilt."

"Like I say," Merrick said, "I think Sam here should start working this idea right away. He knows the players and he knows the town. I want to spend the day looking at all the crime scene data that idiot chief-of-police claims to've collected. He's got one guy on his staff who graduated from the academy in Des Moines and knows something about crime scenes. Hopefully, the chief let him handle all the scientific evidence."

"He probably did," Spellman laughed. "Cliffie was too busy primping for the cameras and telling everybody how he was going to make life safe again here in Dodge City. How the hell'd this guy ever get his job?"

"It's a long story," I said.

Spellman smiled. "I'll bet it is."

Scotty McBain sat outside his shack of an office. The day was too sweet with warm autumn to be inside. He sat in his chair and had his feet propped up on an empty wooden Pepsi case stood on its end. He was reading a Fredric Brown paperback, *The Screaming Mimi*.

"You've got good taste in books."

He looked up and smiled. He's got a small, terrier-like face with a large mouth and easy grin. "Hey, if it ain't the perfesser."

Dad's friends from the plant started calling me that when I got the undergraduate scholarship to the U of Iowa. I was not only the first kid in my family to go to college, I was the first to go down at the plant. Simple reason. I was born during the war. Their kids were born after. They'd

239

be hitting college in a few years.

Scotty wore a faded khaki shirt and trousers. A uniform, like. He took his feet down from the Pepsi case and stood up, touching his hands to his lower back. "I'm gettin' old." Before I could disagree politely, he said, "You can have your pick today."

He nodded to two stacked rows of aluminum canoes set against the front left wall of his office. Most of them were in good condition. A few yards away, the river ran, smelling faintly of fish. Out on the water a red speedboat moved fast and vivid through the water. The small dock he'd built for himself was a spot for keggers during the summer. The men, mostly veterans who worked with Dad at the plant, would play a softball game (it was jokingly called The Very Slow Pitch League) and then end up drinking beer half the night at Scotty's dock. Dad used to take me along sometimes when I was ten or so. I loved the war stories. Even then I knew they were exaggerated for effect but I didn't care. Every once in a while the stories weren't bravado, though, and one of the guys would choke up and start crying, thinking of some friend dead back there in Europe or the South Pacific, and it was funny because it was the only time I'd ever seen a male person cry when the other male persons around him didn't get up-tight or ashamed. Couple of them would go over to the guy and slide their hand around his shoulder and kinda stay there like that till the guy stopped crying. My cousin was like that when he came back from Korea. Up and down the emotional scale a lot. He finally ended up in the bughouse, though nobody in the family ever brought it up. If somebody asked how Tim was doing, Mom and Dad would just say that he was "away for a while."

"No canoes today, Scotty. Sorry. I'm working on something and I was hoping maybe you could help me a little bit."

"Me? Now that's a new one. Some kind of criminal case, you mean?"

"Uh-huh. I'm told there's a woman lives up the road in a trailer. Used to be friends with Karen Hastings."

He frowned. "Ross Murdoch. That boy's in trouble." Stuck a Chesterfield between his lips. "Too bad. He was the only one of those rich guys who was decent. He'd come out here once in a while with his daughter when she was high school age. They were both real nice. Just average people, like. Not puttin' on any airs or anything, not askin' for any special treatment. They'd always go to that little summer house he kept over there on that hill across the bend down there. You can't see it from here. But he enjoyed it, I know that much." He grinned. "Wouldn't be bad, though, havin' a girl as good lookin' as Karen was stashed away somewhere."

"She come down here a lot?"

"Not a lot but four, five times a summer. Janice Wilson was the one who came down a lot."

"She the one lives up the road in the trailer?"

"Uh-huh. Little silver Airstream. Just about right for one woman, I guess. She gave me a beer one day after I worked on her car. Sat inside her trailer. She's got it fixed up pretty good." A smile. "Just like she's got herself fixed up pretty good. She just wore a halter and shorts that day. Tell you, I felt like I was eighteen again. Smart gal, too. Lotsa books in her trailer. A little distant, though, that's the only thing. She's friendly and all but you never feel she's opening up at all. You know what I mean?"

"Yeah."

"S'pose Cliffie'll be checkin' her out, too."

"I suppose." I stared out at the choppy

water. Then back at Scotty. "I hear she's got a temper."

He laughed. "Yep. She sure does. Especially with men who put the make on her real obvious-like. She's strictly look-but-don't-touch."

"Ever see her with anybody except the Hastings woman?"

He thought a moment. "Nope. Don't think so."

"No other girl friends? No male friends?"

"I'll give it some thought, Sam. But off the top of my head, I'd say no. Wasn't like she hung around here or anything."

I looked up the road. "Well, I'll see if she's in. See if she'll talk to me."

He gave me a friendly fake-punch on the arm. "Sure wish I was your age again and got to hang around gals like Janice Wilson. Sure wish I was."

SEVENTEEN

Thirty minutes later, I started making my rounds. Janice Wilson hadn't been in so I decided to get the real scut work over with. I called Mike Hardin in the hospital. He sounded strong and sure on the phone. "The afternoon before Ross found her in the bomb shelter? I'd have to think about it."

I heard a nurse squeak into the room.

"She doesn't think I should talk to you, McCain," he said. "She claims I'm too weak. How do you like that? She's standing at the end of my bed with her hands on her hips. She's got very nice hips." Then: "I just remembered. Hunting. I was hunting. You can check with my secretary, if you'd like."

"Who'd you go with?"

"Go with? I only hunt alone if I can help it. Hunting's something I take very seriously. I hate to spoil it by turning it into a social event. A bunch of middle-aged drunks wandering around in the boonies, that's not my style."

"So you don't have an alibi."

"I don't like the tone of that. If I tell you I was hunting, I was hunting. My secretary knows."

"She knows what you told her."

"You know what? I think this pretty nurse standing at the end of my bed has a real good idea. I'm not going to talk to you any more."

He slammed the phone.

Peter Carlson took my call. "I should tell you, I have a lawyer now." He spoke as if from a great height, the way he did to all humanity.

"You tell your lawyer that you fell in love with Karen Hastings?"

"You don't know what the hell you're talking about, McCain."

"Don't I? And if I'm not mistaken, you roughed her up some, too. I guess that's one way of expressing your love."

"This is all bullshit and if you start spreading it around, I'll sue you for libel."

"Slander. Common mistake. Libel is the written word."

"What is it you want, anyway?"

"Where were you the afternoon before Karen Hastings's body was found?"

"Right here in my office."

"You have witnesses?"

"Several, in fact. We had a staff meeting that afternoon."

"All afternoon?"

"Most of it. We didn't get started till one-thirty. I think I've said all I'm going to now, McCain."

He hung up, too.

He had what seemed to be an alibi but it was one of those that could be taken apart and found wanting, I was sure. If the meeting at the Murdoch mansion was pre-arranged, the killer could have met her there — or picked her up and driven her there himself — killed her and left, all within an hour or so.

When you study trials in law school, you see how many juries are swayed by small lies, particularly alibis. While it sounds reasonable for a man to forget what he'd been doing for two or three hours a month or two previous, it presents a great opportunity for the prosecutor. If the DA can prove that the man did a couple of things he'd almost certainly remember — made a substantial purchase, spent a substantial amount of time with somebody, was involved in a substantial traffic accident — the prosecutor can then say that he finds it odd that the man on trial would forget that. He can also say that the traffic accident incident took no more than forty-five minutes according to the other driver and the cops on the scene — leaving the man on trial with two hours he still can't account for. Where were you the other two hours? You're not going to get a conviction on the basis of these questions but you are going to make the jury wonder if the man is honest and forthright. And he has left the two unaccounted-for hours dangling out there. Trials are mosaics. They rarely have the kind of aha! moments you see on TV.

My final call was to Gavin Wheeler. He was a mite drunk, especially considering that it was barely eleven a.m. "I walk down the street and they stare at me like I'm some kind of monster. Or they snicker. People who always used to speak to me, say hello to me, smile at me. It's like they're embarrassed to see me. All my life I've tried to build up my reputation. I'm not some nobody from the Hills any more. I've got a name, I've got money, I've got some power. Or I had 'em, anyway, McCain. I don't know why the hell I ever got into this thing. My poor wife won't leave the house. She went to the grocery store nine o'clock last night when it was just about closing time. There weren't any customers but everybody who worked in the store stood there whispering about her. A couple of them even made a couple of smart remarks. I did that. Me. All the years she's stayed married with me — and I ain't no prince to live with, believe me — and look what I do to her. We should be thinking of retiring now. But we're gonna have to get clear the hell away from here."

I'd waited him out. "The afternoon before Karen Hastings's body was found in Murdoch's house. You happen to remember what you were doing?"

He had an answer right away. "Driving back from Davenport. Had to look at some property over there."

"Alone."

"Yes, alone."

I could sense that he would be most unhappy if I pushed beyond this point. I didn't feel up to arguing with an eleven a.m. drunk. I said thank you and hung up.

I was just going through my notebook, transferring some of the notations to a larger sheet of paper, when the phone rang.

"I'd like to speak to Mr. McCain."

"I'm Mr. McCain."

"My name's Janice Wilson. Scotty told

me you were looking for me. I need to drive into town, anyway. Why don't I stop by your office in two hours or so?"

"That'd be fine. I appreciate the call."

That's the best way of all, when they come to you.

The Judge has paid exactly two visits to my office. Today was the second one. In her tailored gray suit with the long leather and very dramatic gray gloves, she had the imperious elegance of a fading movie queen. Every move was straight from finishing school, every utterance straight from her upper-class New England education. I'm pretty sure she once gave lessons to Katharine Hepburn in haughtiness.

"You really do need to get better digs, McCain."

"So I hear."

I said this as I walked around my desk, brushed off the better of the two client chairs, and held one out for her. She looked at it as if I'd just bought it at a leper colony garage sale. But she put her important ass in my unimportant chair, lighted a Parliament and dramatically exhaled smoke. She saw the rubber band before I did. A lone rubber band sitting near the edge of my desk. How could she resist picking it up, using her thumb and fore-finger as a bow, and firing it at me the way she usually did? But we were both getting crafty. She pretended not to see it and I pretended not to see her pretending not to see it. She went so far in trying to fake me out that she sat all the way back in her chair and raised her eyes to meet mine.

"I'm here because Deirdre Murdoch asked me to be."

"Deirdre? Why doesn't she call me her-self?"

"She's in a panic now since she found out there'll be no bail."

"No bail?"

"The judge — me — has decided there'll be no bail."

"But why?"

"I'm recusing myself from this whole matter. But until a new judge is selected, I'm not going along with bail. I'm too good a friend of the family."

"So meanwhile he sits in jail."

She paused a moment. I wondered if she was thinking about the rubber band. She loved playing Pearl-Harbor-sneak-attack.

"I came here, McCain, to ask a simple question. I wanted to see your face when you answered it. Irene Murdoch is an old friend of mine. I'm afraid she'll have to go back into the sanitarium."

"I know. Deirdre told me."

"Thank God for Deirdre. Ross was gone so much — the only lasting friendships Irene has had were with me and Deirdre."

"I guess I don't know what your question is."

"It's a very simple question, McCain. Because if I don't get the answer I want, I'll have to start preparing Irene and Deirdre for the worst."

"That being?"

"That being that Ross did commit these murders and will be going to prison."

"And you want to know if I think he's guilty?"

"Exactly. We don't always get along, McCain, but I do have some respect for your word."

I smiled.

"Did I say something funny?"

"That 'some respect' crack. You could've just said, 'I have respect for your word.' You didn't need to hedge your bet that way."

"Shilly-shally. You're just stalling because you don't know how to *answer* my question." Then she smiled. She had a mischievous smile that was almost girlish. "You're getting slow, McCain."

So like a dummy I followed her gaze to where the rubber band had been. I'm emphasizing the past tense here. Because the rubber band was no longer there. It was on its way to my — nose. She shot it with her usual callous skill and now it lay across the bridge of my nose.

"I imagine you feel triumphant," I said.

"No more so than usual where you're concerned."

"This really is quite immature, you know, for someone of your age and stature."

"Oh, McCain, let's not talk about my age and stature. That's so dry. Let's talk about how ridiculous you look with a rubber band lying across your nose. That's a lot more fun."

"You came here just to shoot me with that rubber band, didn't you?"

"My, aren't we the paranoid one today? Yes, McCain, I'm psychic. I knew there'd be a rubber band sitting there on your desk, out in the open as it were. So I hurried over to take advantage of it." Then: "Don't be ridiculous. I came here because I'm concerned about Irene and Deirdre. They've been through so much with him and now this. He's such a charmer that I always forgave him his indiscretions, too —

he's tried to get me into the sack upon occasion, too, difficult as it is for you to imagine, McCain — but I just put it down to the martinis. And now this. This — with that girl — is impossible to forgive. Irene will never recover. I'll say it again, thank God for Deirdre. They've decided to put off going to the sanitarium until tomorrow, by the way. They're both just too tired today."

"I'll put it this way. If I had to bet, I'd bet he was innocent."

"Really? That's interesting. Why?"

"People as smart as he is don't leave bodies in their bomb shelters."

"But maybe that's the beauty of this whole thing."

"What is?"

"He puts the body in there and everybody thinks just what you said — he's too smart to put the body where somebody's sure to find it. A jury would take his status, his history and his intelligence into account and find him not guilty."

"I'm getting a headache."

"Oh."

"This is all getting pretty complicated."

She smiled sweetly. "Perhaps for a tiny brain like yours.

"You really did look funny with that

rubber band hanging off your nose like that. Been a long time since I did that to you," she continued with a smirk as she stood up.

"Not long enough."

"Oh, you crab," she said as I walked her to the door. "You know you like it as much as I do. The little rubber band thing."

"Love it," I said. "Positively love it."

It was just past one. That gave me an hour before Janice Wilson came to my office. I had a sandwich at Rexall. Mary was behind the counter but the place was still packed with late lunchers. Mary and I exchanged, in order, smiles, winks, smiles and melancholy looks because we wouldn't have a chance to talk. I didn't even see her at the cash register. Somebody else took my ticket.

I sat in the park and alternately read through my notebook and watched the squirrels stock away food for the winter. I wished I could be a part of nature the way all the little animals were, a true part of the cycle. Even living in a small town in the Midwest, you are cut off from nature. You get more of a chance to see it but you rarely have the time — or, face it, the inclination — to get into the woods or the prairies or the farm fields and learn about it firsthand. The irony was that the people who spent the most time with nature — excepting farmers, of course — were the hunters, whose pleasure it was to kill a part of it. Life, as my dad always says, is like that sometimes.

I stopped off at a store that sold used items and bought a copy of Budd Schulberg's *Winds Across the Everglades*. Nobody had paid much attention to the book or the movie. But both were lyrical and bloody looks at the destruction of the Florida Everglades as far back as the turn of the century. Just the same way nobody paid much attention now to how Midwestern rivers were being used as toilets by manufacturing plants.

I figured I'd get in fifteen minutes of reading before Janice Wilson showed up.

But she was waiting for me. As soon as I pushed through the glass outer door, I saw that my office door was open about an inch. I'd left it that way in case she beat me here. Through the crack between door and frame, I saw the back of a blonde head with the collar of a blue suede jacket turned up.

I had to get all the way into my office before I realized that she wasn't doing anything. Even when you're sitting silently, you tend to move a bit, scratch your chin, run a hand against your hair, shift your position, unconscious, nervous mannerisms that everybody has.

She wasn't moving.

I walked around her chair and looked down at her.

She was a very dignified-looking working-class girl. The white ruffled blouse and blue skirt and blue hose and blue one-inch heels were tasteful but cheap. The thigh-length suede coat was a notch up. The matching suede purse was stitched badly and the pieces hadn't quite fitted together. But there was nothing cheap about the face. It was one of those long, earnest, solemn faces that bespeak hard work, honesty and intelligence. Well-scrubbed. Perfectly made up. Not quite beautiful but quietly sexual.

There was blood on the right side of her head. Fresh blood. Her breath came in little bursts, almost asthmatic-sounding.

I rushed to the john and soaked up half a dozen paper towels. I took a pint of bourbon from my desk drawer and poured three fingers into a glass. The booze is for clients. It's in the private eye's list of Things To Have In The Office. I have yet to get a fedora or a trench coat but I have no doubt they'll be coming along soon.

"Somebody hit me."

"They sure did."

She'd come awake like Sleeping Beauty. Wide blue eyes trying to remember who and where she was. Dry, full lips parting to speak sleepily. Confusion, fear, and finally recognition all playing silently across her appealing womanly prairie face.

"You're McCain."

"I'm McCain."

"It was dark in your doorway there. I think I caught somebody trying to get into your office. They really let me have it."

"Apparently."

She spidered long fingers across the area of the wound. "I don't think I'll need stitches."

I handed her the glass with the bourbon and then tapped two aspirin out of a bottle. She took both gratefully. She shuddered once after ingesting the aspirin. Then she began sipping the bourbon.

"Should I call the police?"

"No. That's why I came here. So I wouldn't *have* to talk to the police. I just want to tell my little story and leave town."

I went behind my desk, sat down, took out my notebook and grabbed a pencil.

"She hated him, you know."

"I guess we need to back up a bit, Janice. Who hated who?"

"Who hated whom, actually. I got A's in English in high school."

"Good for you, Janice."

She smiled for the first time and it was worth the wait. She was like right out of the box at Christmas time — shiny, fine, immaculate. "I always correct people's grammar."

"Endearing habit."

This time the laugh was throatier. "You don't hide your irritation very well."

I smiled. "I'm sorry. You're sitting here with a lump on your head and I'm being less than gentlemanly. My apologies. Now how about your story."

"Well, let me try to organize it. I guess the simplest way to say it is that Karen Hastings used to come into the Embers in Cedar Rapids. I grew up on a farm near Cedar Rapids and started taking night classes to get a college degree. The tips were good at the Embers and I liked the people so I've been there for three years. I've got two years of college behind me now. Anyway, Karen always came in and ate. She was so beautiful I could see why she'd attract all her men. Then I started to see that she kind of rotated through four different men over and over. There was a pattern there. And they ran to a type. Twenty years older, obviously well-to-do, and very taken with her. Sort of courtly, in fact. She was like the pretty little girl that all the uncles wanted to shower with gifts. The funny thing is, she always looked lonely. I guess I picked up on that because I'm the same way myself. I have a lot of opportunity for dates but most of them just make me feel worse than better. The guy I was seeing is in the Marines. Last winter they sent him to Vietnam. Have you ever heard of it?"

"I know we're sending more and more troops over there is about all."

"Anyway, so I'm lonely and she's lonely and one of the nights she came in alone, she asked me if I wanted to have a drink after I got off. That's how we got to be friends. The place she lived in — I'm a farm girl, I'd never seen any place like it. I'd never seen a sports car like hers, either. She didn't ever say it — she wasn't much for talking about herself at first — but I caught on that these men were keeping her somehow. I wasn't sure of the arrangement right away but it got to be clear. And then they started getting jealous of each other."

"Anyone in particular?"

"Carlson?"

"Peter Carlson?"

"Yes. I was in her apartment one night when he started banging on the door. She was terrified of him. We had all the lights off. But he was so drunk, he just kept pounding. I asked her why didn't she call the police? Later that night she explained her arrangement with the men. I could see why she couldn't call the police. Then she started hearing from her brother. The first time I met him I couldn't believe they were even related. Quiet little guys like that I usually feel sorry for. But not him. He scared me. He was four years older than she was. She told me he used to force her to have sex with him all the time they were growing up. He wasn't as meek and mild as he liked to seem. Anyway, what he wanted her to do was start shaking down these men. He knew that with Carlson acting the way he was, the whole thing was going to come apart very soon. But he saw the opportunity with Ross Murdoch running for governor to really collect one big blackmail payment. He said that since he'd set this whole thing up he was entitled to half of it."

"Did he ever threaten her?"

"Oh, sure. A lot. She was afraid of him. She told me that she'd tried to hide from him several times — she lived in New York and Miami twice each — but that he'd found her both times."

"Was she planning to run away this time?"

"I think so. But I'm not sure." She paused. "She didn't want me around any more. When I called, she'd get me off the phone as quickly as possible. And the same when I saw her on the street one day. She said she was busy. But I could tell that something else was going on."

"But you didn't know what?"

"No, I'm afraid I didn't."

"How long did this go on?"

"Oh, a month or so I'd say. Obviously something had happened."

"Did she seem scared?"

"Not exactly. More like anxious, I guess. But not scared. I even asked her about that, if there was anything I could help her with. She just said no and then got off the phone right away."

"And you have no idea what she was doing?"

"Afraid I don't."

From the center drawer of my desk, I took the restaurant receipt. Handed it over to her.

She smiled. "I've seen several thousand of these over the years."

"Take a closer look at it, would you? Her brother put some significance on this that I haven't been able to decipher."

She studied it. "The date — I was in Chicago that whole week. I had a lot of vacation saved up."

"So that isn't your ticket?"

"No. The initials for the waitress are CG. That'd be Callie George. Very nice young woman. And there's a 10 in the upper right hand corner."

"I noticed that. What's that signify?"

"What we call a 'friend' discount. If you wait on a relative or close friend, you're allowed to give them a ten per cent courtesy discount."

"You think there's any way Callie might remember who this ticket was written for?"

"Well, it might be her friend or my friend. We switch stations a lot. I take hers on her nights off and she takes mine. So we pretty much know each other's courtesy discounts. I can ask her when I see her today. I'm on my way to work now. I can call you from there if you want me to."

"I'd sure appreciate that." Then: "This has sure been helpful."

"Well, I guess I was right to be worried, anyway. She always thought she was so — tough, I guess you'd say. That's one of the reasons she was so interesting to be around. She always had all these little plans going. You know, ways she could take advantage of this person or cheat that person, things like that. Never big things. Never like robbing a bank or anything. And I was fascinated. I thought she was sort of cool. But then the more I got to know her — she started to scare me. I'd always assumed she was putting on the toughness to some degree. But she wasn't. She really enjoyed tricking people. And that's when I started pulling back."

"But you kept calling her."

"You're going to laugh."

"I could use a laugh."

"I was trying to get her to go to this Bible class I take once a week. I got dumped by this guy — and this class saved my life. I'm not a real religious person but it gave me some perspective. I thought maybe it would help her, too. I planned to arrange it so we'd go on separate nights. I didn't want to see her any more. But of course she wouldn't go. She just thought the whole thing was a joke. She said, 'God, you really *are* a farm girl.' She'd always said that I wasn't as unsophisticated as I thought." She shrugged. "We didn't end up very well. I still feel sorry for her, though. Having a brother like that —" She checked her watch. "Well, I need to get to work, I guess." She stood up, offered a slim hand. We shook.

A few days ago, I would've thought about asking her for a date sometime. She looked bright, earnest and sweet. But somehow as we'd been talking, I began to realize my need to be with a woman. And the woman who kept coming to mind was Mary.

I saw Janice Wilson to her car and said good-bye.

EIGHTEEN

There was another gathering downtown. On the steps of the Catholic church. No candles because it was daylight. Everybody in kind of a hurry because it was the end of the day and home sure did sound good. The spouse, the kids, the food, the TV, the furnace kicking in and sounding good and smelling good as it did so — heat having its own very particular smell — no wonder they said there was no place like it.

Again it was a cross-section of people, the old woman wearing the bulky winter coat she'd bought ten years ago, thread-bare now; the young businessman in his camel's hair topcoat and white silk scarf; the day laborer with his Oshkosh winter jacket, the collar lined with union buttons; the prim middle-class housewife in her smart royal blue dress jacket and dark blue jaunty hat; and the ancient Negro man, a face rutted and ruined by so many small losses and humiliations and modest dashed dreams that there had to be a few moments here and there when the notion of nuclear destruction didn't sound all that bad.

A priest today, not a minister, a young and modern-minded one who wore a black turtleneck instead of a Roman collar, jeans instead of trousers, and played a guitar instead of read from the Bible, a Woodie Guthrie song I liked just fine except that I didn't see its relevance here, given the occasion I mean, the world maybe going to blow up soon.

But that was my problem. I sit in a courtroom and mentally wander off about where I'll have supper tonight. I sit in a church and think not of Jesus but about what comely ankles the woman in front of me has, which I happen to notice right below me whenever we're kneeling down. Or I stand in front of a church and play music critic, thinking not of the holocaust that might soon befall us but of what a poor choice of songs the young priest chose for the occasion. I'm a regular pip, I am.

There were probably two hundred people here. There'd been no word from the Russians. Everybody was in a "what if" mode. What if the Russians did this, would we then do that? And so on.

The ceremony ended with everybody singing the Our Father, the priest leading us in the Protestant version because this was a Protestant town and he wanted to be polite, which was understandable.

As I walked back to my office, I heard somebody groan behind me. It was a very particular sounding groan. More like a moan, I guessed. I'd heard one like it only once before. When my Uncle Bill was having a heart attack.

I turned to see Abe Leifer again, only this time he was grasping at his left arm and starting to pitch forward to the sidewalk. His face was dead pale. His mouth was opening to scream but he had neither the time nor the strength for it. He grew whiter by the moment.

We were near the corner, where there was a police call box mounted on the support column of the street light. I ran to check Abe first.

Then I was shouting at a farmer in a John Deere cap, "Use that call box! Get an ambulance!"

He looked confused at first. Then he looked as if this might be some sort of gag, with a cameraman hiding somewhere. *Candid Camera*, the show that trapped people into doing dumb things and filmed them doing them.

I was no expert at mouth-to-mouth but I gave it a try.

Beth Leifer sat on one side of her mother and I sat on the other. This was the waiting room outside the surgery.

Helen Leifer would be all right and then she would not be all right. Beth was a pretty, thirtyish woman with intelligent gray eyes and a smile that was as gracious as a papal blessing. Her husband Del and I shot baskets a lot on the outdoor court at our old high school. Beth wasn't smiling now, of course. She was trying to keep her mother in an optimistic mood. I was pretty sure she was trying to accomplish the same thing with herself. The doctor, a man named Fred Knowles, was big, cold, gruff. He'd interned with Himmler.

There was a clock down the hall. Abe had been in surgery more than an hour now.

I said, "I'm going down the hall to the bathroom, Beth."

"We'll be fine. Take your time. Get a cup of coffee if you like."

"Would either of you like one?"

"I'd sure appreciate one. Mom can share mine."

"I'm not even sure I could hold down coffee, the way my stomach feels." Helen and Abe had been married forty years. Impossible to imagine what Helen was going through now.

On the way to the cafeteria, I passed the Volunteers office. I saw Peggy Leigh, the volunteer coordinator I'd met the other day. I waved to her. She waved me into the office. She was behind her desk, talking on the phone.

I roamed the small room. One wall was covered with photos of various volunteers, including the candy-stripers. Deirdre certainly looked fetching in her crisp nurse-like blue-and-white uniform.

Next to this was a board that listed the monthly schedule for the candy-stripers. I looked at Deirdre's name. She sure put in a lot of hours here. But as I started to note the particular hours, something didn't seem right. I was still studying them when Peggy Leigh said, "How would you like to be a celebrity for a night, Sam?"

"I gave up tap dancing years ago." I turned away from the scheduling board.

She smiled and I knew she was on a mission to get me to volunteer for something.

"Tuesday nights, we have guest speakers come to the cafeteria and give a little spiel to the patients who're interested. You being an investigator and all, I'm sure they'd be fascinated."

"You know, Peggy, now that you mention it, I *am* a pretty fascinating guy."

"C'mon, Sam, I'm serious. You could probably tell a lot of stories about your work."

"Names changed to protect the innocent, of course."

"However you want to do it."

"Could I do it next month?"

"That'd be fine. Second Tuesday all right?"

"Barring anything unforeseen."

"My daily horoscope said this was going to be my lucky day."

"I'll probably have to make stuff up, Peggy."

"Sure, Sam, sure."

Her phone rang.

I nodded goodbye and went and got two coffees and brought them back to where the Leifers sat in the waiting room.

We drank in silence. Helen seemed to have shriveled inside her massive storm coat. Beth was starting to show the effects, too. Tears in her eyes. Hands trembling every once in a while. I tried to think of something to say. There wasn't anything.

I'd never gone through this kind of waiting before. But someday I'd have to, just as some day somebody would be waiting on me. Wife or child. Maybe my kid sister Ruthie if we ever lived in the same town again. There's something holy about this kind of grief, the grief of waiting. Everything is cleansed but for the love you feel. The terrible wonderful holy *burden* of the kind of love that binds you forever to a particular person.

We sat through a shift change, some down-the-hall radio reports on the missile crisis that didn't seem to be abating, and numerous offers of food from nurses.

The doctor came out at about seven o'clock. He'd undergone a personality transplant. He was almost tender now. He spoke mostly to Helen, as was appropriate I suppose. "Things are looking a lot better now. He suffered a heart attack but it wasn't as critical as we first thought it was. I'd say his chances for recovery are very good and without any kind of permanent damage. We'll have to raise some hell with him, Helen, about those donuts he likes so much."

She smiled through relieved tears. "The donut shop is right next door to his business. It won't be easy."

He took her hand and then Beth's. "You can see him in a little while. What I'd suggest now is that you two go down to the cafeteria and have some supper. I'll talk to you in the morning again."

He nodded to me and walked away, long, quick strides.

They both hugged me. I hugged them back.

"Say a prayer for him, Sam, please."

"I will, Helen. I promise."

Beth kissed me on the cheek. What nice soft lips.

I grabbed a couple of burgers and a Pepsi and ate in my office. In ten minutes, I got two calls. The first was from the Judge.

"There's something funny going on, McCain."

"And that would be what?"

"That would be Ross Murdoch getting out of jail on bail and then disappearing."

"You mean jumping bail?"

"I'm not sure what I mean other than the fact that Irene Murdoch called me and is very frightened. She said she'd never seen Ross the way he was this afternoon when he got home from jail. She said he acted as if he was in some sort of stupor.

Deirdre said she thinks he's suffering from terrible depression about everything."

"And I'm to do what?"

"Start looking for him."

"He's free to do what he wants, Judge, as long as he doesn't leave town."

"McCain, listen. I told Irene I'd get back to her. I want to tell her that you're looking around town for him and I want that to be true."

"I thought Irene was going up to that hospital for a while."

"She was. It's sort of a retreat for her. She just goes up there when things get too much for her. But she refused to leave until she heard that bail had been arranged. She wanted to be there when Ross got home. That's when she got scared."

"Well, I'll look around. But don't hold out much hope. If he wanted to disappear for a few hours, I'm sure he can find someplace where I'll never find him." Then I remembered something Scotty McBain had said. "Doesn't he have a summer house?"

"Oh, a little one. Nothing fancy. They bought it when they first got married. I don't think any of them has spent much time there since Deirdre was a little girl."

I asked her for directions and she told me.

"Call me in a couple of hours and let me know if you found anything," she said.

I went to the john and freshened up. I needed more coffee and I was nearly out of cigarettes. I kept a sweater folded neatly in the bottom drawer of my desk. A black crew neck that clashed with very little. I was sick of the necktie and suitcoat. I slipped on the sweater and was headed for the door when the phone rang again.

Janice Wilson was on the line, "I talked to the other waitress. She remembers Karen Hastings coming in that night. She was with another woman. She can't remember anything about her. She said that one of the busboys actually served the meal and wrote up the check, they were so busy. She said that all she did was initial it so Karen could get the discount. That isn't very helpful, I'm afraid."

"Another woman. Well, at least we know it wasn't with one of the four men."

"Sorry, Sam. I've got to run. I'd like to see you again sometime, if you're ever interested."

"Very interested. Thanks for the call."

Other woman, other woman, other woman. You know how the echo machine plays the same phrase over and over again in a movie character's mind? Mine was sort of doing that on the drive to Ross Murdoch's summer home.

The problem was that the woman could easily have been just an acquaintance who had nothing to do with Karen's eventual murder at all. I'd half-suspected her dinner guest was her brother. I'd thought maybe they were making last minute preparations for their final blackmail payment. The big one.

The wind was hard enough to make my ragtop sway side to side on the deserted blacktop road that led to the woods commonly called Peer's Peak after the man who'd had a huge apple orchard out here for decades. The land behind his was thorny forest that dropped down to the river.

In the headlights, the black night looked bleak, the cold ebon river was touched by cold golden moonlight, and on the other side of the road steep timber rose to form one wall of a canyon. The river people lived out here year-round in shanties and shacks and tiny trailers. Every couple years, they got flooded out but they always came back. It was a hardscrabble life, their TV antennas and silver propane tanks and junker cars being their most valuable inanimate assets. It was one of those nights so dark you nearly suspected that dawn would never come again, that the dark forces at play in the cosmos had finally banished daylight forever. At the moment it was even impossible to remember what sunlight looked like.

I found the off-trail road the judge had described. I got out and took down the wooden crossbar and drove through the gate. I got out again, put the crossbar back in place and began the narrow, winding, strange trip into forest so deep it seemed to absorb the beams of my headlights. This time of year, autumn leaves covered everything. I kept the driver's window down, my .45 right on the seat next to me. There was still enough wary kid in me to know that I was in the heart of an evil land. A cop I knew once told me that any time you found deep forest you'd find a human body or two that had been buried years ago and was now little more than dusty bone. If you were so inclined to spend your free hours digging. Not a pastime I'd care to indulge in.

Wooden shingled one-story house with a screened-in front porch and a steeply pitched roof. The grass was a couple of inches tall and the forest was starting to reclaim the backyard area. Ross Murdoch's black Cadillac sedan was parked in front. My headlights gave the house a lurid bleached look, the way those photos look in true crime magazines.

I switched off the ignition, grabbed my .38 and flashlight and got out of the car. The wind off the river, which was behind a screen of birches, was hard cold. The stench was of fish.

I went to the side window and poked my flashlight right up against the glass. Murdoch hadn't even tried to make it resemble any kind of hunting or sport cabin. It was furnished in solid middle-class New England furniture. Ethan Allen from the looks of it.

I saw nothing out of place. But I also saw no evidence of Ross. Had he gone for a walk? Was he maybe asleep in the bedroom?

I went back to the front door. Took out my handkerchief and proceeded to make my way inside without leaving any fingerprints. I stood in the living room and flipped on the wall light. Everything was dusty, including the 21-inch Admiral table model TV. The screen was opaque with dust. I called out his name several times. My voice sounded alien to me in the gloom.

A door opened on a spring that needed oiling. Then slammed shut.

The kitchen. I ran through the alcove at the other end of the dining room, straight into the dark kitchen. I flipped on the overhead light. Standard issue, like the rest of the house. Newish but dusty stove-refrigerator-counter-cupboards. The kitchen had an empty feeling to it, like a stage kitchen in a TV commercial. Open the cupboards and you'd find nothing more than mice droppings. Open the refrigerator and you'd see nothing but empty metal racks.

All this — the run through the dining room, my assessment of the kitchen — took less than half a minute. I hurried out the back door that somebody had just let slam.

The warm sweat from inside turned to frozen sweat in the cold night. Maybe ten yards separated back yard from woods. I shone my flashbeam at the dusty wall of hardwoods. There were three narrow paths between four widely separated trees. Each seemed to angle off in a sharply different direction.

I heard something, or thought I heard something. But by then it was already too late.

I was struck from behind with more violence than had ever been visited upon my head before. I'd been punched hard, struck glancingly with a piece of sturdy wood, even kicked just above the temple. But never anything like this. This was the sky falling on me.

I doubt I remained conscious for more than two seconds. There was this spike of pain that obliterated all other senses, a spike that tore through my head front to back like a bullet. And yet I somehow knew I hadn't been shot. Something else. . . .

And then there was just the darkness. I'm sure I didn't help myself any by slamming my head against the frosty ground. But at least I didn't feel it for longer than a millisecond. . . .

Pain. Stabbing pain, numbing pain, blinding pain, pain from which there was not a moment's escape. My senses seemed to switch on one by one. A car in the distance trying to pull away, slamming into gear, scraping a tree — hearing. The hardwood wall I'd seen before being knocked out — seeing. The cold ground, dead grass scratching my cheek — feeling. But they were all faint senses and impressions. Nothing could be as strong as the unyielding, throbbing pain.

I think it took something like two weeks to lever myself to my feet. I know I dropped to my knees a few times in the process. Then I saw the clothesline pole and crawled over to it. Good old clothesline poles. They never let you down. I wrapped my arms around it and began to pull myself to my feet. Good old clothesline pole. I hung on to it like a drunk in an old vaudeville sketch hanging on to a street light.

I stood there a good long time. I wasn't sure if the pain lessened or I was simply adjusting to it. Still a raw bitch of malice and mendacity and torture. But not quite as bad as it had been when I'd first come to.

I managed to light a cigarette. And after a few minutes I saw the rock. It took me a few more minutes to reach it, to grasp it in my hand. It was the size of a hardball but jagged. One edge of it had a healthy sampling of my hair, blood and scalp on it. A perfect weapon.

I let it drop to the ground and then I turned to face the house. I needed to go back in there and finish looking around. Maybe my assailant had left something behind.

I moved carefully, trying not to generate more pain.

The lights were out. I went into the darkness. The door of a small metal fusebox was open in the kitchen. I was able to see what my assailant had done. Had run out the back door, circled around to the front of the house, come back inside just as I was leaving, pulled the fuse from the box and got rid of it, and then eased outside where he launched the rock. The Cubs could use a pitcher this good.

I finished looking through the house with my flashlight.

There wasn't any shock when I found him. I'd pretty much expected to find him. I couldn't tell you why. Just some sense of where this whole thing was going, all the information of the past two days starting to assume a recognizable shape.

I found Ross Murdoch sitting on the toilet with the lid down. I was glad that my beam was narrow. I wouldn't have wanted to see it all. He'd used a .38 and a good half of his head was adhered to the wall behind him in patches of hair and slime and streaky splashes of blood. What remained of his head was angled to the right, resting on his shoulder as if his neck had been snapped in some remarkable way. The gaze of the dead eyes was a roadkill gaze — that awful look of eternal shock and terror you see on possums and raccoons and squirrels that have been run over.

His right arm was flung across the sink. The .38 dangled from his finger.

I looked around for a note he might have left, even though I was pretty sure this hadn't been any suicide. No note, of course.

I looked for footprints, fingerprints, smudges, anything that would help tell the story of what had happened in this bathroom. The *roomness* suddenly got to me. The ghosts of it. Pretty ladies daubing on makeup in the mirror above the sink. Adulterous men taking nervous stock of themselves in the same mirror. Women crying, drunks trying to sober up with face splashes of ice-cold water, somebody being sick. And now this dead man. This would alter the small room forever. The energy of it, those ghosts that record every single moment of every single room they haunt.

I went to the kitchen and worked on my wound as well as I could. It hurt like hell to touch it even with a warm wet rag. I sat down and smoked another cigarette and consciously tried to gather myself. There was no phone. I would have to go back to town to find one. I'd put the top down. I'd freeze but it would sharpen my senses.

There wasn't any point in looking at him again. There wasn't any point in staying around. There wasn't any point in denying the thought that had been taking shape since I'd been in Peggy Leigh's office earlier — and since I'd gotten the phone call from Janice Wilson. That Deirdre could easily have left the hospital at any time during her scheduled hours — and come back without anybody noticing. Especially if she moved quickly enough.

As I pulled away from the front of the summer house, I remembered the sound of a car that had been pulling away as I'd lain there with my head smashed in. I put on my high beams and crawled along the narrow road slowly, examining every foot of the road on either side of me. I was nearly at the end of it before I saw what I needed to see.

I stopped, got out, went over to where a car had angled between two widely spaced trees to hide in deep undergrowth. It had been a rough entrance and an even rougher withdrawal. The whole area looked as if a piece of heavy equipment had smashed it down. I could still smell the fumes of the gasoline needed to push the car through the nearly impenetrable undergrowth.

I spent several minutes examining brush and trees alike. There were two places where you could see that the car had scraped up against a coarse surface. I took out my Cub Scout knife and took a sample of the scrape and then set the sample inside my handkerchief.

I put my flashlight beam on the scrape. Easy enough to see who the car belonged to. The same yellow paint on a certain little foreign car.

NINETEEN

I found a phone booth next to "Your Cheatin' Heart," a honky-tonk visited at least once a week by cops and an ambulance. Them there boys do like their fightin'.

I called Spellman and told him what I'd found and what I'd figured out. He argued against what I had planned next. I told him to give me an hour. I told him this was the best way, the surprise method. He still didn't like it but he agreed to an hour, at which point he was calling Cliffie if he didn't hear from me otherwise.

A man in a black leather jacket and a face shiny with blood came staggering out of the door along with his equally drunken pal. A country singer with the unlikely name of Ferlin Husky wailed on the night, accompanied by some very nice picking on the slide guitar.

The man's friend, who was walking along next to him, said, "Tried to tell you she was his wife, dummy. That's why he got so mad."

"All I did was grab her tit. I didn't even grab both of 'em."

I could hear this one in court. *Your honor, my client grabbed but one of her tits, not both. I ask you, is a one-tit-grabber really a menace to society?* Judges are very sympathetic, as you know, to such brilliant pleas.

I made up some pretty good speeches on the drive out there. The accusation, the denial, the final confession. My parts in them, anyway. She'd have to come up with her own and I was sure she would.

I was beginning to understand it, the motive I mean. Maybe I was even a little sympathetic about it.

I'd been spared the kind of household atmosphere she'd grown up in, so I couldn't judge her. I might have reacted the same way. I had a friend whose mother had an affair years ago and it seemed to have had a permanent effect on every member of the family. The husband was never quite able to forgive the wife; the wife was bitter because the husband would never acknowledge how many times he'd let her down before she had the affair; and the three kids had to listen to their mother being called a whore a couple times a week. They also had to minister — like ambulance drivers — to whichever parent was in the more mental anguish at the moment. They went on to have terrible marriages themselves, the kids. Too glibly Freudian to say that this was because of what they'd gone through with their own parents — but then it must have given them a pretty dark and scary view of marriage.

The lights were on. I knocked. I waited two minutes. No response. I rang the bell. Two minutes. No response. And then suddenly the door was opening and she was there.

If she suspected why I was here, she disguised it well. "I'd say winter's not far away."

"It sure isn't."

"It's good to see you. C'mon in."

I followed her inside.

She wore a white blouse and black slacks. Her bottom was tops. She had put a red ribbon in her dark hair, the red of it matching the rich red of her lipstick. A little touch of the exotic.

"Anything to drink, Sam?"

"No, thanks."

"Any news?"

"Not anything you don't already know."

I think she knew, then. Our eyes met, held.

"Listen to the wind, Sam."

We were in the den. She was fixing herself a drink at the dry bar. I'd declined. She kept her back to me.

"Autumn wind always sounds so lonely, don't you think, Sam? Like a little girl crying."

I was standing. Now I sat. "A little girl crying because her father was rarely home. A little girl crying because her father spent all his time with other women. Driving the little girl's mother into depressions so bad that she had to be hospitalized."

She still hadn't turned around. "Sounds like a novel you're writing."

"The father would have left them but he wanted to be governor someday. No way a divorced man would ever be governor in this state. Somehow the girl found out about her father's indiscretions — maybe stumbled across some letters; maybe eavesdropped on a phone call, could've been a number of ways — and realized that this was what was destroying her mother. The mother got worse and worse. The girl pleaded with her father to give up his women, to live a decent life. But the father just kept right on living the way he always had. And the girl grew up hating him for what he'd done to her mother. She didn't care about herself and what he'd done to her. Her hatred made her strong. All she cared about was her mother and how she'd been destroyed. The girl was strong. The mother wasn't."

She walked from the dry bar to the leather couch that faced my leather chair. She sat down, put her head back against the chair, closed her eyes.

She was right about the wind. In the silence you could hear a child crying. A lonely little girl, say — a lonely little girl who didn't really care much about the fact that she was attractive and rich and clever. She just wanted her mother to be happy. That was all.

She closed her eyes and tilted her head back against the chair. "I don't suppose it was all that difficult to figure out, was it, Sam?"

"Not after I realized that you'd found out about the blackmail money Karen Hastings wanted. And about the relationship she had with your father and those three other men. You had dinner that night at the Embers with Karen Hastings, didn't you? I imagine that's when you told her how much you were afraid of a scandal and that you'd pay her what she wanted even if the men wouldn't. A week later you called her and told her to come to your house and collect her money. You killed her in the basement and put her in the bomb shelter. You knew everybody would think your father killed her. You didn't want to prevent a scandal. You wanted to create one. You knew that when the body was discovered, the whole story would come out and he would be destroyed. You wanted him to suffer. And you pulled it off, kiddo. He suffered all right. He was a scandal and a dirty joke and he'd never be able to walk down the streets of this town again without somebody smirking at him. Of course, walking down the street was sort of a moot point, wasn't it? He'd be in prison for murder."

We listened to the wind some more.

"You going to say anything?" I said.

"Nothing to say, Sam."

"What made you decide to kill him tonight?"

Her eyes were still closed. Her breasts rose and fell with her soft sighs. I imagined that she'd spent a lot of sad hours like this, trying to shut out the world.

"Deirdre?"

"Do we have to talk, Sam?" Then: "I read this story once. About this little girl and all these terrible things happened to her. But then somehow she figured out that she was just part of a dream the man upstairs was having. The entire universe existed only in his mind. She was miserable and so was everybody in the world. So she went upstairs with a butcher knife and killed him."

She was silent for a time.

"Then what happened, Deirdre?" I said softly.

"Then there was just — nothing. She didn't exist because the terrible man couldn't have his terrible dreams any more."

"That's pretty sad."

"Maybe not, Sam. Maybe it was better that she didn't exist. That nobody existed. Then they couldn't hurt each other or betray each other."

She began to cry, then, in little spasms of delicate grief. "Why don't you just call the police, Sam, and we'll get it all over with."

"I can give you a little more time."

"No, Sam." She sat up in the chair and looked at me. "Please. Now. We'll just get it over with."

I called all the people I needed to call, including Cliffie, and then went over to the bar in the den and had a drink. I went to the bottom of the stairs twice and shouted up to Deirdre. I doubted she'd try to escape. She answered both times.

There were two cop cars. Cliffie came on his motorcycle. All three had sirens blaring. The first contingent of press wasn't far behind. Cliffie had obviously called them.

He came up to me where I stood on the steps, in the glare of patrol car headlights. He'd had time to put on his white Stetson and his swagger.

"I figured it was her all along," he said.

"Sure you did. That's why you arrested her father."

"Ever think I was trying to set a trap for her?"

"The mind boggles," I said.

"Where the hell is she?"

"I'll go get her."

He turned and waved at a cop with a shotgun. "Earle, get over here." To me he said, "Earle'n me'll go inside with you."

I couldn't fault the police procedure but I knew why he was doing it. So he could bring her out on the porch personally. In handcuffs. His hand on her arm. Cliffie Sykes, Jr. Bad-ass.

"All right," I said.

"Nice of you to give me permission and all," Cliffie said.

I couldn't tell you today which came first, the scream or the gunshot. I don't believe I'd ever heard a scream or a gunshot that sounded quite as loud as these did. They seemed to paralyze everybody for long seconds.

And then Cliffie, Earle and his shotgun, and I were running inside to the staircase. Cliffie and I reached the first step at the same time. I pushed him out of the way and took the stairs two at a time.

The weeping guided me to the master bedroom. The door was closed. I flung it open. What I saw didn't make sense at first. Deirdre's mother hadn't gone to the hospital after all.

Irene sitting on the chair of her enormous makeup table, her face in all four mirrors. She wore a simple blue dress. Her right hand was on the table and in her right hand was a large handgun. Above her there was a large oval crack in the ceiling plaster. A snowfall of the stuff was all over her hair and shoulders.

Cliffie damned near knocked me down

getting into the room. He had his gun drawn.

The weeping came from Deirdre, who was in a chair by the fireplace. Curled up in a fetal position.

The other cops were crammed in the doorway, watching.

Cliffie said, "You take your hand off that gun, Missus. You're just gonna make everything worse for everybody. I came here to arrest your daughter for murder. And I'd advise you not to get in the way."

She didn't do it right away. Instead, she just looked up at him. I had a sense that she was lost to reality for all time. There was a sadness about her that you see in the faces of the hopeless on the wards of mental hospitals. They're so sedated they walk zombie-style down the halls, slippers slapping, heads down.

She lifted her hand from the gun and said quietly to me, "I killed all three of them, Sam. Deirdre realized this tonight when I took her car and went out to the summer house." She raised her regal head to Deirdre, still in the chair. "She's protected me all her life. While I was the one who should have been protecting her. I was selfish. I should've divorced Ross a long time ago. Deirdre would have been so much better."

294

She glanced down at her large, muscular hands. "They were terrible people, Sam. Terrible people." Then she went on to explain that Kevin Hastings had tried to blackmail her directly and showed her the Embers receipt and told her he knew what was going on. And then she saw a way to destroy them all — expose the men for what they were, rid everybody of the Hastingses.

Then she looked back at me. "I killed them, Sam. Not Deirdre."

And I knew she was telling the truth.

TWENTY

Half a day after Washington announced that a deal had been struck with Russia, that Khrushchev would be dismantling the missile sites, there was a party in the park. A sure sign that it's a real true community party is when very old people dance. And dance they did. There was a polka band and that was their muse. Other sure signs of a true community party were free burgers, free potato salad, free pop, free beer. The youngest teenagers raced around the park performing antic pranks, while the older teenagers flirted, or yearned to flirt, or hung out with kids who weren't afraid to flirt. It seemed like every woman there had an armload of babies, bouquets of babies. The men from wars past played horseshoes and smoked corncob pipes or Luckies or Camels and talked about how Jack Kennedy had redeemed himself from his invasion of Cuba.

Late in the afternoon a bunch of kids, all of whom tried to look like either Elvis or

Buddy Holly or eerie amalgams of both, replaced the polka band and swung into rock. This brought out little ones as wee as three and kids of eight and up. I did all my dutiful dancing with cousins somewhere around my age. In small towns, you were expected to. They'd been fine for dunking in pools, beating in races, locking in closets, scaring the hell out of in dark rooms, laughing at the first time you ever saw them in makeup or high heels, even have useless idle *verboten* crushes on from time to time. Now it was time to act like a grown-up and dance with them. One of them was pregnant, one of them was drunk, one of them was gorgeous and one of them listed eight things I'd done to her over our mutual childhood that she still planned to pay me back for, including dropping an Ex-Lax tablet into a Pepsi.

For these hours, euphoria — which had to be going on all over the world — euphoria triumphed in Black River Falls, Iowa. Sundown came with a clear and melancholy beauty, with even some of the very oldest dancing to Buddy Holly songs . . . and people who didn't usually speak to each other there were talking with Pepsi and Pabst cans in their hands.

The world had been spared the worst

war of all. And for these exquisite hours we were bound up, each of us, in our common humanity.

I was finishing off a Pepsi when I felt fingers on my arm. I turned and saw Mary who said, "How much would you charge to dance with me?"

I looked at that shy sweet face, that face I'd been looking at since we'd had our kindergarten photo taken together, and said, "This is your lucky day, ma'am. Sam McCain is having a sale. For you he's absolutely free."

"Well, that sounds reasonable enough."

"It sure is good to see you, Mary."

She laughed, taking my hand. "Shut up and dance, Sam."

A ballad would've been nice. But even bopping to "Great Balls of Fire," it was romantic as hell anyway. Because everything was romantic at this moment in the history of old planet Earth. Everything.

ABOUT THE AUTHOR

Ed Gorman has been a full-time writer for more than two decades, his work appearing in nine different languages, his novels "providing fresh ideas, characters, and approaches" according to *The Oxford Book of Crime Fiction*.

Though Gorman has written in several genres, he considers himself primarily a suspense writer and primarily a novelist, though he has several short story collections to his credit, one of which won The International Fiction Writers Award, attesting to his reputation in Europe.

Over the years, Gorman has also written radio and television scripts plus nine feature length movie scripts. His collaborative book *The Haunted* became a much-acclaimed television movie.

His work has won praise from such diverse sources as *The Bloomsbury Review*, which called Gorman "the poet of dark suspense"; *Kirkus Reviews*, which acclaimed him "one of the most original crime writers around"; and England's *The Tally*, which characterized his books as "intelligent, literate, mature and compassionate. And he writes some very attractive prose."

Gorman lives in Cedar Rapids, Iowa, with his wife the writer Carol Gorman, his four grandchildren, and three cats.

We hope you have enjoyed this Large Print book. Other Thorndike, Wheeler or Chivers Press Large Print books are available at your library or directly from the publishers.

For more information about current and upcoming titles, please call or write, without obligation, to:

Publisher
Thorndike Press
295 Kennedy Memorial Drive
Waterville, ME   04901
Tel. (800) 223-1244

Or visit our Web site at:
www.gale.com/thorndike
www.gale.com/wheeler

OR

Chivers Large Print
published by BBC Audiobooks Ltd
St James House, The Square
Lower Bristol Road
Bath BA2 3SB
England
Tel. +44(0) 800 136919
email: bbcaudiobooks@bbc.co.uk
www.bbcaudiobooks.co.uk

All our Large Print titles are designed for easy reading, and all our books are made to last.